MYSTERIES SOLVED

25¢ a day plus expenses

murders extra

Call G. O'Brien Private Eye   222-2323

Gabby was going to be a private eye. There was a mystery out there just waiting to be solved, and she was going to solve it.

She got her coat from the hall closet. It was her winter coat. But it had a belt. It was the closest thing she had to the kind of coats private eyes wear.

She poked around in the closet, found her summer-camp hat, and put it on, pulling the brim low over one eye. She looked at herself in the hall mirror.

She really did look like a private eye.

TO
CATCH A CROOK

DOROTHY HAAS

A MINSTREL® BOOK

PUBLISHED BY POCKET BOOKS

New York   London   Toronto   Sydney   Tokyo

This book is a work of fiction. Names, characters, places and incidents are either the product of the author's imagination or are used fictitiously. Any resemblance to actual events or locales or persons, living or dead, is entirely concidental.

 A Minstrel Book published by
POCKET BOOKS, a division of Simon & Schuster Inc.
1230 Avenue of the Americas, New York, NY 10020

Published by arrangement with Clarion Books

ISBN: 0-671-67240-1

First Minstrel Books printing April 1989

10 9 8 7 6 5 4 3 2

A MINSTREL BOOK and colophon are registered trademarks
of Simon & Schuster Inc.

Printed in the U.S.A.

For Ruck
Remembering the sunny, laughing days.

Contents

TO CATCH A CROOK

1

"Gotcha, Gabby O!"

"**I** know what I'm going to be," Gabby whispered to Amy. "A private eye."

"I'm going to be a veterinarian," Amy whispered back.

"Ha!" muttered Justin, who sat in the desk behind Gabby's. "Girls can't be private eyes."

"Says who!" Gabby swung around, forgetting to keep her voice down.

"If you please, Gabrielle," said Mrs. Cole, turning away from the chalkboard. "Let me finish. You may talk on your way home."

She dusted chalk from her hands and looked around the classroom. "Now, you all have a full week to get ready for Career Day. Go to the Learning Media Center. Find out what tasks will be part of the work you choose. Next Friday we will give our reports in class. You may bring samples of your work to show – "

The bell sounded in the hall.

" – to the class if you wish," said Mrs. Cole, her voice rising as everyone started stuffing books into backpacks.

It was the first really warm day of spring and everybody rushed to get out of school. Gabby stopped on the steps to pull off her jacket and tie it around her waist. Without her jacket, with the warm air on her bare arms, she felt free enough to fly. She jumped down the steps.

She and Amy walked home together, talking about veterinarians and private eyes. Amy knew just which part of the Learning Media Center had books about animals.

"I don't need to go to the LMC," said Gabby. "I've seen lots of private eyes on TV. I know what I need to do."

"Hey, Gab." It was Justin. He and Bucky were walking behind Gabby and Amy. "Like I said, you can't be a private eye."

"Why can't I?" Gabby demanded, glaring at him, her fists on her hips.

"Because who's gonna rescue you?" Justin snickered. "I mean, when the bad guys capture you or you fall in the lagoon at the park?"

Gabby felt her face getting hot. "Justin," she said softly, firmly, "why don't you go play in the traffic?"

Justin cackled. "Gotcha!" he said. He always said that when he made her mad. "Gotcha, Gabby O!"

Gabby sent Amy a disgusted look that said as plain as words, "Justin is a pain."

Just then Bucky pushed one of his round, thick, felt-tip pens close to Gabby's lips. "Hello," he said. He made his voice deep. "I'm Thomas Bucks from Channel Fourteen. Tell our viewers what you think of Career Day."

"It'll be fun," said Gabby. "Maybe not the report, but what leads up to it. I mean, the stuff I'm going to do this week."

"I'm going to investigate news stories this week," said Bucky. "Listen, Gab, if you solve a mystery, let me know. I'll interview you on my tape recorder."

"Not *if* I solve a mystery," Gabby said patiently. "*When* I solve one. And yes, I'll sure tell you."

"I've got a mystery, sort of," said Amy. "My mystery is, how can I be a vet when I can't have a dog or cat? I mean, Tommy wheezes when he gets near fur."

"How about a bird?" asked Bucky.

"Feathers," said Amy in a gloomy voice. "Tommy wheezes."

"Goldfish," said Justin. "They haven't got fur."

"You can't hug a goldfish," said Amy.

Poor Amy. She had a terrible problem with her little brother. Gabby wished she could fix things for her. "How about a turtle?" she asked.

"We had one once," said Amy. "It was kind of fun. But it wasn't very loving. Sometimes its bowl smelled terrible. After a while it got lost. My mom found it under the refrigerator. But she wouldn't let me look at it. After that we didn't have a turtle anymore."

"Maybe you can be something else," Justin said helpfully.

Amy got her stubborn look. You had to believe Amy when she looked like that. "A vet," she said. "That's what I'm going to be."

The soft, blurry sound of rolling wheels came from behind them. Gabby turned.

Porter was coming along the sidewalk on his skateboard. It wasn't like any skateboard in the whole world. It had a motor. Porter held the cord in his hand and pressed a button that made the motor run. The skateboard moved smoothly along. He didn't have to push with his feet at all.

"Hey, Por," called Bucky. "What're you going to be?"

Porter looked confused, as though he were coming back from the middle of next week. He seemed to see them for the first time. He stopped. "What?"

"You know," said Bucky. "What Mrs. Cole was talking about. What're you going to be someday?"

"Oh." Porter returned to his private world. "An inventor," he said as he rolled away. He looked like a statue moving down Chilling Street, his head high, his eyes fixed on some wonderful plan only he could see.

"Porter's a genius," said Bucky, watching him. "He put that motor on his skateboard. Will you look at him move! Wow!"

"He took apart his dad's tape recorder and put it back together when he was six," said Gabby.

"He put a motor on the fuzzy bunny he got for Easter when he was four," said Amy.

"He's absent-minded, too," said Justin. "Geniuses are supposed to be like that. But hey – his head isn't very big. Don't geniuses all have these really big heads? So maybe he's not really a genius."

They all stared at him.

"Justin," said Gabby, "that's the dumbest thing I ever heard. You're a real airhead."

"Gotcha!" Justin laughed maddeningly. "Gotcha!"

Gabby groaned and turned away from him.

"I wonder what Porter will invent next," said Bucky. "If I can get him to come out of his fog, maybe I can tape an interview with him for Career Day."

"Gab," Amy asked, "how are you going to find a mystery to solve?"

"Well, first I'm going to let everybody know I'm – I'm – " Gabby hunted for the right private-eye word. "I'm *available*," she finished proudly. *Available* was a good word. Private eyes used it all the time on TV. "I'm going to advertise."

Amy looked impressed. "You mean like in the newspaper?"

"Or on TV?" asked Bucky. "Hey, I can be the announcer."

"If you need an actor," said Justin, "I can be him. I was a pretty good gorilla in the Valentine's Day play."

Gabby looked at him thoughtfully. "Justin, I've got the perfect part for you."

"You have?" Justin looked hopeful. "Do I get to wear a gorilla suit or something?"

"You get to be the dead body," said Gabby. And she didn't even say *Gotcha!* She was above such childish things.

2
Murders Extra

The bedroom door was closed and the key was turned in the lock. Gabby's little sister was out in the hall banging on the door. "Let me in," she yelled.

Nicki was a monster. Gabby sighed. What had happened to the darling toddler she and Mom and Dad used to have so much fun with?

"What's on the sign on this door?" hollered Nicki.

Gabby knew what was on it. It said "Private Eye — Keep Out." She held up the ad she had just finished making.

MYSTERIES SOLVED
25¢ a day plus expenses
murders extra
Call G. O'Brien Private Eye 222-2323

It looked pretty good, even if she did say so herself.

The banging on the door changed to a slow, heavy thudding. Gabby knew what Nicki was doing. She was lying on her back on the floor, her feet in the air, kicking the door with her heels.

"What are you doing in there?" screeched Nicki. "It's my room, too."

Gabby looked around. Ads lay everywhere – on the dresser, on the beds, on the floor. Every ad she made was better than the last. She wished she could throw away the first ones. Some of the letters were crooked. And she had left the E out of *murders* on some of them. But the ads were hard to make. She couldn't throw any of them away. She needed them all.

The noise at the door changed. It wasn't Nicki's kind of thumping. It was an I-mean-business grown-up knock.

"Gabrielle," called Mrs. O'Brien, "open this door at once."

Gabby put down her felt-tip pen and pushed her dark hair away from her face. She got up and turned the key in the lock.

The door banged open and Nicki burst into the room. "You're using my side of the room," she yelled. "Get your dumb stuff off my bed and off my floor." She grabbed the ads from her bed and threw them at Gabby.

"Don't wrinkle them!" wailed Gabby.

"That will do, Nicole." Mrs. O'Brien stood in the doorway. "Don't muss your sister's schoolwork."

Nicki still held one of the ads. "What does this say?" she asked.

Mrs. O'Brien came into the room, carefully stepping around the ads. "There's no need to lock the door. Perhaps if you gave Nicole some small job when you want to do your schoolwork, she would be quiet."

"WHAT . . . DOES . . . THIS . . . SAY?" roared Nicki.

Mrs. O'Brien winced. "Read it to your little sister," she said.

Gabby read one of the ads. "I'm going to put them in people's mailboxes," she explained.

"You're going to catch crooks," said Nicki. Her eyes were bright with interest. "I'll help you." She smiled sweetly.

"Mo-therrrr," Gabby moaned.

"Dear," Mrs. O'Brien said to Nicki, "I'm going grocery shopping in a few minutes. Why don't you come with me?"

Nicki looked like she wasn't sure she wanted to do that.

"You can choose the cereal," said Mrs. O'Brien.

That seemed to sound interesting. "Any kind I want?" asked Nicki.

"Almost any kind," said Mrs. O'Brien. "But not one that's half sugar."

"And can I get a Kitty Nose?" asked Nicki. "One with whiskers and a rubber band to hold it on my face?"

Mrs. O'Brien sighed. "Kitty Nose," she agreed.

"If you're going to get a Kitty Nose for Nicki," said Gabby, "can I have a — "

"Gabrielle" — Mrs. O'Brien's voice was soft — "don't push your luck."

Gabby was quiet. Nicki was going to be out of her hair. That's what she really wanted.

Nicki followed Mrs. O'Brien out of the room. Then she poked her head around the door. "Kitty Nose." She said the words silently, with great big movements of her mouth. She grinned at Gabby before she ran to catch up with Mrs. O'Brien.

Gabby sighed. She had been doing a lot of sighing about Nicki lately. Nicki was acting. . ."Spoiled," Gabby thought. "We're spoiling her."

She was going to have to talk to Mom and Dad about Nicki.

She finished piling the ads in a stack. This was the best assignment Mrs. Cole had given them all year. Imagine! Schoolwork that was heaps of fun! She was going to be a private eye. There was a mystery out there just waiting to be solved, and she was going to solve it.

She got her coat from the hall closet. It was her winter coat. But it had a belt. It was the closest thing she had to the kind of coats private eyes wear.

She poked around in the closet and found her summer-camp hat on the floor behind the folded-up card table. It was green and it had a kind of brim. She brushed a dust kitty off it and put it on, pulling the brim low over one eye. She looked at herself in the hall mirror.

She really did look like a private eye.

She picked up her ads and set out to deliver them.

3

Gabby the Gumshoe

All of the bushes had big, fat, ready-to-burst buds. The first feathery leaves made clouds of pale green high in the treetops. Warmed by spring sunshine, Chilling Street was a busy place this Saturday morning.

Mr. Bashaw was on a ladder cleaning the gutters on his roof.

Mrs. Chung was raking old brown leaves from under the bushes in front of her house.

The Clifton twins were digging up a flower bed while their mother stood near, telling them how to do it.

Miss Haliber was pulling weeds from among the tulips near her front steps.

They all watched Gabby put the ads in their mailboxes and said they would read them later.

Cutting back and forth across the street, Gabby had given out more than half the ads when Amy rolled down her driveway on her bike. She dropped the bike, went to see what Gabby had put into the mailbox, and came to walk beside her. "Do you think somebody around here is going to be murdered?" she asked, reading.

"You never know," said Gabby. "Private eyes have to be ready for anything."

"What does this mean" — Amy pointed at the ad — "expenses."

"Someone has to pay for things that cost extra," said Gabby. "Private eyes always say that."

"What kind of things?" asked Amy.

Gabby didn't answer until she had stuffed an ad into the Petersons' mailbox. "Well," she said, coming back to Amy, "just suppose I'm tailing somebody and he ducks into Cinema Two. I have to follow him there. I can't just wait in front — he might go out a side door. So I have to buy a ticket to get in. That's an expense."

"Wow!" Amy was impressed. "You'll get to see a lot of movies before they're on TV."

"Not if the suspect" — Gabby liked that word — "sneaks out before the end."

Amy's eyes widened. "That would be terrible. You wouldn't see how the movie turns out."

"It goes with the territory," said Gabby.

Bucky and Justin came out of Bucky's house. Bucky had his tape recorder. "I'm going to interview Mr. Oakley," he said. "I'm going to ask him why he keeps the Christmas tree lights on the trees in his yard all year long."

Justin tugged at one of the ads folded over Gabby's arm.

"What've you got there?"

She let him have one of the ads. He and Bucky looked at it together.

"Hey, Gab," said Justin. "You spelled *mysteries* wrong."

"Ha!" said Gabby. She knew what Justin was up to and she wasn't going to give him a chance to Gotcha! her again. "Ha!" She didn't even look at the ad.

Justin grinned at her.

"Do you go in for missing persons — I mean missing animals?" asked Bucky. "My caiman has disappeared."

"You mean that little alligator — "

"It's not an alligator," said Bucky. "A caiman's different. It's its own kind of animal."

"Okay," said Gabby, "your caiman. The one your uncle gave you for your birthday?"

"The same," said Bucky. "But hey! You wouldn't charge a buddy a quarter a day, would you?"

Gabby wasn't sure she wanted to find the caiman. To be honest, she was a little afraid of it.

Amy wasn't. "Poor little thing," she said. "I wonder what it's finding to eat."

Gabby bit her lip. Private eyes took whatever work came along, even if they didn't like it. "I won't charge a buddy anything, Bucky," she said. "I'll help you find the caiman. Only I'll have to do it after I work on my other cases."

A truck from the Green Thumb Garden Center stopped ahead of them. A man got out and carried some shiny metal planting boxes to the McCabes' porch. He rang the bell, but nobody was home. He left the boxes on the porch and stuffed an envelope into the mailbox. Gabby put her ad in with it.

"Got to go now," said Bucky when Gabby came back to the sidewalk. "Gimme an ad, Gab, and I'll put it in the Oakleys' mailbox for you."

He took the ad and went up the walk, fiddling with his tape recorder, talking into it, "Testing, one, two, three. . . ."

Amy ran after him. "Bucky," she called, "do you suppose your caiman is hiding under your refrigerator?"

"Listen, Gab," said Justin in a voice oozing with kindness, "you just let me know when you need help." He grinned maddeningly at her and headed toward the corner.

Gabby sizzled. "Justin," she called, "you – you – "

Justin turned. "Gotcha!" he cackled, walking backward and into a sagging carton of soggy brown leaves. He sat down with a thud. The sides of the box burst and the leaves spilled onto the sidewalk.

Gabby doubled over, laughing. "You are such a klutz, Justin," she said between gasps.

"Agreed," said Mrs. Tanaka from her front yard, smiling. She was leaning on her rake. "I think you owe me a new box to put those leaves in, Justin."

Justin stood up, brushing off his jeans. "Yes, ma'am. I'll bring you one when I come back from the mall." He eyed the pile of leaves at her feet. "I'll bring you two," he said good-naturedly, turning to go.

Mrs. Tanaka laughed. "But I think you'd better change your pants first. You're all wet from those leaves."

Justin felt the back of his pants. His ears turned red and he ran toward home.

Gabby grinned, watching him scurry down the street. For once, Justin Abrams had been caught by one of his own Gotchas!

Mrs. Driscoll's house was set far back from the street. In front was a garden with bushes cut to look like animals — an elephant and a bear and a seal. At one side was a little pond with a bridge over it. Beside the bridge was a sign that said "Beware of Trolls."

The gravel path didn't lead straight back to the house. It wound in and out among flower beds. In the center of the garden was a shiny silver ball on a pillar. Gabby put her face close to the ball. Her nose became huge and her eyes and mouth slid back from her nose. She grinned at herself, and that was funny, too. The silver ball was the best thing in Mrs. Driscoll's garden.

She found Mrs. Driscoll around a curve in the path, pulling weeds from among some daffodils.

"Hello, Gabrielle," said that pleasant lady, sitting back on her heels. She pulled off her gloves and wiped her forehead with the back of her hand. "My goodness but it's warm for this time of year. Aren't you hot in that coat?"

"This is my private-eye coat," said Gabby. She held out an ad. "I solve mysteries."

Mrs. Driscoll read the ad carefully. "What a lot of fun," she said brightly. "You're playing detective."

Playing! Gabby felt her face get red. But she answered politely. "I'm going to be a private eye someday and I need all the practice I can get now. This is part of my school-work," she added as an afterthought. "For Career Day."

"Schoolwork." Mrs. Driscoll took that seriously. "I see." She folded the ad and put it in her pocket. "Well, dear, I don't come across many mysteries. But if I do, I'll certainly call you."

She picked several daffodils. "Here, dear. These are for you."

Gabby headed back to the street, admiring the yellow flowers. They were like sunshine in her hands.

On the sidewalk once more, holding the daffodils awkwardly, she folded her last ad. She left it in the mailbox of the house on the far corner. The house was empty, but maybe someone would move in soon. Then she headed homeward to put her daffodils in water.

The O'Brien telephone was busy that night. First Amy called. "Has a murder happened yet?" she asked.

Mr. O'Brien came through the hall. "Don't make a marathon of it," he whispered.

Gabby didn't have time to tell Amy much except that she had asked if she could take karate lessons in case she ran into a big, tough crook. "My mom said no and it's about time for me to take *dancing* lessons."

Amy groaned. "She'll talk to my mom, and if you have to, so will I."

Parents were, they agreed, hard to live with.

The phone rang again during the station break between "Hired Gun" and "Aliens." Gabby leaped to answer it. She said hello just as Mr. O'Brien picked up the extension in the den.

"Hey, Gab." It was Bucky. "Mr. Oakley says he turns on the lights – "

"Excuse me," said Mr. O'Brien. "I just want to remind Gabby that there's a two-minute limit on the telephone tonight."

The extension clicked.

Gabby wanted to die. It was so embarrassing when parents said things like that in front of your friends.

"I'm sorry, Bucky," she said. "I guess my dad is waiting for some big-deal phone call."

Quickly Bucky told her about the lights. "He thinks they're pretty."

"Well, they are," Gabby agreed. Mr. Oakley was probably the only person in the whole world who turned on the Christmas lights in his yard for all the important days — July Fourth and Lincoln's Birthday and Hannukah and Halloween and Chinese New Year and Valentine's Day. He had even turned them on for Gabby's last birthday.

"It's sort of a news story," said Bucky. "I'll play the tape on Career Day — unless a better story comes along. Have you got a mystery yet?"

"It's still only Saturday!" said Gabby. "Something will happen before next Friday. You'll see."

"I-believe-you, I-believe-you," said Bucky.

Mr. O'Brien answered the phone the next time it rang. He listened for a moment. "How are you, Jean. . . . Yes, she's here at my elbow."

He covered the mouthpiece with his hand. "It's Jean Haliber. Grownup or not, keep your call short."

Gabby took the phone. What could Miss Haliber want to talk to her about? "Hi, Miss Haliber. This is Gabby."

"Gabrielle, my umbrella is gone. I'm sure someone took it."

Why was Miss Haliber's voice shaking like that?

"I'd like to hire you to find it. I'll be glad to pay your rate of twenty-five cents a day."

Miss Haliber sounded really funny. A terrible suspicion rose in Gabby's mind. Was Miss Haliber laughing?

"Gabrielle, are you still there?"

"I'm here," said Gabby.

"Well, will you take my case?" asked Miss Haliber, and now her voice sounded perfectly normal.

She couldn't be laughing.

"I'll take your case," Gabby agreed. Her first case! "Can I come talk to you about it tomorrow afternoon? We go to church in the morning. And then we're eating lunch at Mario's Cafe and maybe we'll stop in the park afterward for a ride on the pedal boats at the lagoon if they're out."

"Any time after lunch will be fine," said Miss Haliber. "I'll expect you."

Gabby hung up. She stood at the phone smiling. Wow! A real case to solve. Then suspicion returned to darken a corner of her mind: Had Miss Haliber been laughing?

She needed to talk this over with Amy. She started to dial the number.

Mr. O'Brien came into the hall. "No more," he said. "I'm expecting a call from a client."

Meekly Gabby set the phone down. But she couldn't keep her good news to herself. "I just got my first case," she said proudly.

"Well!" Mr. O'Brien ruffled her hair. "My daughter the gumshoe. Congratulations!"

Gabby felt really good.

4

A Real, True Mystery

Gabby usually loved eating at Mario's. But not today. She shared a pizza with Nicki, and her own half only had cheese and olives and onions with no meat on it. They had bubble-gum ice cream for dessert, too. But lunch seemed to last forever.

Later, they drove homeward through the park. As they got near the lagoon, Gabby saw that the pedal boats were in the water again, after the long winter. The first ride of the year was what Gabby always called a Big Moment. But today all she could think about was getting home and talking to Miss Haliber. She bounced with impatience.

Mrs. O'Brien turned around in the front seat. "Shall we stop for a — " she started to say to Gabby. Then her eyes rested on Nicki. Nicki had fallen asleep. "Ohhhhh." Mrs. O'Brien looked sorry. "I know I promised you a boat ride, dear. But maybe we should just go on home and let Nicki sleep."

Gabby was big-hearted about it. "Sure, Mom. If we wake her up now, she won't take a nap at all and she'll be crabby later."

And if Nicki had her nap now, there wouldn't be a problem with her following Gabby around.

Mr. O'Brien carried Nicki into the house and put her into bed. She partly woke up and fussed and said she didn't want a nap, she wanted to help Gabby catch crooks. . . . Her eyes closed halfway through *crooks.*

Gabby escaped without waking her. Stopping only to put on her private-eye coat and tug her private-eye hat low over one eye, she slipped out of the house. She headed down the block to Miss Haliber's, pulling the belt of her coat tight.

Her footsteps slowed as she neared the tall, yellow house with its orange door and dark green shutters. But her heart speeded up. Her very first case!

Miss Haliber was washing out the birdbath as Gabby rounded the corner into the backyard. She watched Miss Haliber turn the hose to a fine spray, filling the shallow bowl. Miss Haliber was blond and pretty. What did it feel like to be pretty? Gabby wondered if she would be pretty when she grew up.

Miss Haliber dropped the hose and pulled off her garden gloves. "My goodness. Aren't you hot in that heavy coat? You can take it off and we'll sit in the sun."

No way was Gabby going to take off her private-eye coat!

She got out her notebook and pencil and sat on the edge of a garden chair.

"When did you notice your umbrella was missing?" she asked in a businesslike voice.

"It looked like rain Friday morning," said Miss Haliber. "I wanted to take the umbrella to the office. But I couldn't find it. It wasn't in the closet, or the hall, or in my car."

"Did you look in the garage?" asked Gabby. "Maybe it fell out of the car."

Miss Haliber shook her head. "It's really nowhere around here. And so when I found your ad in my mailbox about the game you're playing, I thought maybe someone took it, and I – "

There it was again! Miss Haliber's voice had that strange shaky sound. Her lips quirked up at the corners. She was laughing. She *was* laughing.

Gabby's face turned red. "I'm not playing a game," she said, coming down hard on that last word. Didn't grown-ups know she was too big for little-kid games? "I'm going to be a real private eye someday, and I'm going to find a case to solve this week for Career Day, and – "

"Oh! I've hurt your feelings." Miss Haliber looked downcast. "Oh, I'm so sorry. I just thought it would be fun to go along with a game, and I forgot how I felt when I was your age, and I – " She bit her lower lip. Then she smiled. "I really do want you to find my umbrella. Let me tell you why."

She moved to the edge of her chair. "I bought that umbrella in Europe. I got it in London, foggy London. That umbrella got rained on in England and Ireland and France. How many umbrellas do you know of," she asked, "with that kind of history?"

Gabby couldn't think of a single umbrella at her house that had anything but American rain on it.

"I'm sorry, Gabrielle," Miss Haliber said again. "I didn't mean to tease or make you uncomfortable. I really do want your help. Now, let me tell you everywhere I've been this past week."

Gabby made a list of the places in her notebook. She described the umbrella. Black, she wrote, with gold handle.

Miss Haliber took Gabby's pencil and drew an umbrella with a twisty handle and a braided tassel. "The tassel is silk," she said, "so it's shiny. Do you think you can find my umbrella?"

"I find my mom's car keys all the time," said Gabby, closing her notebook. "Last week I found my dad's magnifying glass. I'll find your umbrella. You'll see."

If Gabby could have whistled, she would have as she left Miss Haliber's yard. She felt full of fizz, as bubbly as a bottle of soda pop. She was going to start checking the places on her list right away.

She started toward Amy's house to tell her about the umbrella. Maybe Amy would want to go looking for it with her.

Activity down the block caught her eye. What was going on at the McCabes'? Mr. McCabe was carrying suitcases into the house, and Mrs. McCabe was on the porch. She was waving a piece of paper and talking a mile a minute to Bucky's mother.

Curious, Gabby went to see what was happening.

"There are supposed to be four," Mrs. McCabe was saying as Gabby came up the walk. "I ordered four of these planters. This bill in the mailbox says the Green Thumb delivered four. But there are only two here."

She pointed at two long, shiny boxes standing on the porch.

"I do seem to recall something on your porch yesterday afternoon," said Mrs. Bucks. She frowned, thinking. "But for the life of me I can't remember how many planters there were."

"I remember," said Gabby.

The two women turned to look at her.

"I was delivering my private-eye ads yesterday," said Gabby. "You've got one there." She pointed at the ad in Mrs. McCabe's hand, underneath the bill from the Green Thumb. "I saw the Green Thumb man put four boxes on your porch."

"Oh." Mrs. McCabe's eyebrows went up. "Now, aren't you alert! That gives me something to go on when – "

"Mrs. McCabe?" Gabby tried to interrupt.

Mrs. McCabe talked on, like a stream tumbling down a mountainside. " – when I call the Thumb tomorrow morning and ask them whatever – "

"Mrs. McCabe?" Gabby spoke louder.

" – is going on. The least they could have done was – "

"Mrs. McCabe," said Gabby, her voice loud, speaking fast, "I'm a private eye and I can find your missing planting boxes. Just read my ad. It's right there in your hand." She pointed.

"Oh." Looking down, Mrs. McCabe saw the ad under the bill. She unfolded it, reading. "You're a private eye. What a fun game. I remember – "

Hastily, Gabby explained about Career Week. "I sure would like to solve your case of the missing boxes."

"Well, I suppose there's no harm in letting you try," said Mrs. McCabe, "as long as you understand that I'll be talking to the people at the Green Thumb."

"I do understand," Gabby said happily. "Just you wait and see. I'll find those planting things for you."

Mrs. McCabe didn't have a chance to answer.

"Gabby! Gabby!"

Amy came running across the lawn.

"Wait till I tell you!" she called. "I've found a real, true mystery for you. Mrs. Driscoll's silver ball is missing. The one," she panted as she came near, "in her garden. I think you better go see her."

"My word!" said Mrs. Bucks. "We seem to be in the middle of a crime wave."

Gabby's head was spinning. Was there a crook somewhere nearby right now, looking out at them from behind a tree?

She didn't have time to think about that interesting possibility, because Bucky came sprinting along the sidewalk on his bike. He made a wild turn into the driveway and skidded to a stop. "Hey, Gab," he yelled, "I think you better get over to Mr. Oakley's. Boy, is he mad! Some of the lights are missing from his trees. Maybe it's a mystery you can solve."

Suddenly there were more mysteries on Chilling Street than Gabby could ever have hoped for. And she was going to solve them all!

5

The Victims

Gabby didn't even say good-bye to Mrs. McCabe. And she didn't walk to Mr. Oakley's house — she ran. Maybe there were other private eyes in town. She wanted to be sure she was the first one to talk to the victims.

Mr. Oakley was in his yard with his sheepdog Bluff and he was hopping mad. Sparks seemed to fly out of his blue eyes, and his bushy white brows stuck out every which way. He led Gabby to a bush beside the front steps.

"Look here! Somebody took all the lights off this bush. But they didn't even touch that one." He pointed.

Sure enough, the bush on the other side of the steps still had its lights.

Gabby studied the two bushes. She was puzzled. "I wonder why the crook didn't take them all," she wondered aloud. Then she had a thought. "Maybe he's planning to come back tonight to take the others!"

Mr. Oakley looked even more fierce. "He'll have Bluff to deal with if he comes back. I'm chaining Bluff on the porch from now on."

Amy and Bucky had followed Gabby to Mr. Oakley's. Amy was alarmed. "But he'll get cold. I wouldn't want to stay outside all night!"

Mr. Oakley laughed. "Not Bluff. Just look at all that hair. The dog's a canine floor mop."

Bluff shook himself as though he knew they were talking about him.

"Bluff won't be cold," said Mr. Oakley. "And he's got a bark that would stop Dracula in his tracks."

Bluff proved it. He let out a couple of barks that rattled the windows on the front of the house.

"Quiet, boy," said Mr. Oakley. "Save it for anyone who comes hanky-pankying around the yard."

"Mr. Oakley," said Gabby. "I'm a private eye. Will you let me solve your mystery?"

Mr. Oakley turned those bright blue eyes on Gabby. The frizzly brows came together in a frown. "I remember your poster," he said.

"My ad," Gabby corrected him. "I don't charge a lot — just twenty-five cents a day plus expenses."

Mr. Oakley considered this. "Any experience?" he asked.

"Almost," said Gabby. "I mean, I've got a couple of other mysteries to solve."

"I drive a hard bargain," said Mr. Oakley. "That's how I got ahead in business. What if you don't find the lights? Do I still pay your fee?"

"I'll find them," Gabby said positively. "I get results." She had heard that on TV. And anyway, she wasn't going to think about *not* getting results.

"Tell you what," said Mr. Oakley. "If you find my lights, you get the full fee — twenty-five cents a day."

"Plus expenses?" asked Gabby.

"Plus normal expenses," said Mr. Oakley. "But if you go cracking up any cars in high-speed chases, I don't — "

"Mr. Oakley!" Gabby couldn't help laughing. "I don't know how to drive!"

Mr. Oakley didn't even smile. "In that case, plus expenses. But if you don't find the lights, I pay you only half the fee. Is that a deal?"

"It's a deal," Gabby agreed. They shook on it and Gabby headed for Mrs. Driscoll's house.

"How much is half of twenty-five cents?" asked Amy.

"Twelve and a half cents," said Bucky. "Hey, Amy, you better catch up on fractions."

"How's Mr. Oakley going to pay Gabby half a penny?" asked Amy. "There's no such thing."

"He won't have to," said Gabby. "Because I'm going to find those lights. You'll see."

They found Mrs. Driscoll planting pansies around the

pillar that yesterday had held the silver ball. She looked as though she might start to cry at any moment.

"The garden club gave me the globe . . ." Her voice wavered. She stopped as though she couldn't bear to talk about it. Then she took a deep breath. ". . . last year. It was first prize. The club is coming to see my garden on Saturday. Oh, I must have the globe. Without it, the garden is like a party table without a centerpiece."

Gabby understood what she meant. All the paths in the garden led toward the center, where the silver ball was supposed to be. Only now the paths led to the empty pillar.

Mrs. Driscoll's plump face was pink. She looked miserably unhappy. "To think," she murmured, "someone would come into this little Eden and commit a crime like this." Her eyes became shiny.

Gabby spoke quickly, before Mrs. Driscoll could cry. "I'll find the silver ball for you, Mrs. Driscoll. I'm a private eye."

"She really is," said Amy. "She even advertised."

"She's got a bunch of mysteries to solve," said Bucky.

Mrs. Driscoll came out of her unhappiness. She seemed to see, really see, Gabby for the first time. "Oh, Gabrielle. Yes, I remember your ad. I'll be reporting the theft. But if you want to hunt for the ball, I'll be glad to pay whatever you charge. How much did you say that was?"

Mrs. Driscoll looked so sad, sitting there on her heels in her spring garden with no silver ball in it, that Gabby had to say something fast to make her feel better. "Oh, I won't charge you anything, Mrs. Driscoll. I'll find it for you, and before Saturday, too. You'll see."

Mrs. Driscoll smiled then. Deep dimples appeared in her rosy cheeks. "Why, thank you, dear. That's lovely of you."

A pleasing warmth filled Gabby. She was relieved to see the smile and the dimples. Mrs. Driscoll just wasn't Mrs. Driscoll without them.

Justin joined Gabby and the others as they came out of Mrs. Driscoll's yard.

"Just got home from the mall," he said. "Last night my mom said either my gym shoes went or I had to move out of the house. My dad said that was going pretty far – he'd buy me new ones."

Hopping on one foot to stay ahead of them, he stuck out the other foot so they could admire the shoe on it. It was bright green with white stripes and Velcro straps.

"You know," he said, walking on two feet again, "the guy who sold them to us said if I don't win the first race I run in these shoes, the store will give back the money we paid for them."

"My gosh, Justin," said Gabby. "That's great." Then she thought about it. "But if all the kids who buy those shoes all win races . . . how . . . can . . . the . . . store. . . ." Her voice faded.

Justin watched her, a super-interested look on his face.

No! thought Gabby. Oh, no! She'd done it again! "Justin?" she said. "Jus-tinnnn?"

"Gotcha!" he said, howling, bending over and slapping his knee. "Hey, Gab, your face is turning red. You better check your oil."

"You!" said Gabby, "you – " She didn't finish. She would not give Justin Abrams the satisfaction of seeing how mad he made her. She bit her tongue, opened her notebook, and pretended to read it.

"Justin, you missed the best afternoon," Amy said as they turned into Gabby's yard. "Gabby's got some mysteries to solve. She really is a private eye."

"Yeah," said Bucky, "and she's gonna get paid, too."

Just hearing Amy and Bucky talk made Gabby forget about silly old Justin. She had four real cases. And she had almost five whole days to solve them.

They all sat on the back steps. She went indoors and got Eskimo Pies out of the freezer.

After a while, Nicki came out of the house. She was red-cheeked and quiet after her nap. Not talking, she sat beside Justin. He let her have a bite of his Eskimo Pie. Pretty soon she was leaning against him and not bothering Gabby at all.

While everyone talked, Gabby wrote in her notebook:

1. Mrs. McCabe's crook took two planting boxes. Why didn't he take all of them?

2. Mr. Oakley's crook took lights off just one bush. Why didn't he take the lights off both bushes?
3. Will the crook come back for more lights?
4. Is the silver ball real silver? Is it worth lots of money?
5. Don't forget the umbrella.

It would be easy to forget about the umbrella, now that she had so many exciting cases. Lost umbrellas weren't very interesting. But private eyes did all kinds of jobs. So she was going to find the umbrella.

Then she got to thinking about the crooks. Did they know each other? Were they, maybe, a gang? Did they have a hideout? Was that where they kept all their loot? Were they sneaking around Chilling Street this very minute, looking for something else to take?

A shiver ran down Gabby's back as she glanced around the yard, half expecting to see a crook hiding behind the lilac bush or darting behind the garage. But she didn't see anybody.

6

Hoot and Annie

Gabby still had lots of private-eye things to do. But how was she going to get away without Nicki tagging after her?

"Amy! Hey, Amy!" A voice carried into the backyard. Amy's little brother Tommy came dashing around the corner of the house. "Grandpa and Grandma are here. They brought you a present."

Amy leaped up. "Got to go home!" she said, following him and calling, "What is it?"

"I'll give you a hint," he said. "It's gold."

Nicki went indoors and came outside with one of her books. She hung on Justin's arm. "Will you read to me?" she begged.

Justin grinned and opened the book. "Once upon a time there was a robin," he read.

"Not robin," said Nicki. "Once upon a time there was a *worm*."

"If you know the story," Justin said reasonably, "why do you want me to read it to you?"

"Because it's my very favorite book in the whole world," said Nicki. "Read!"

"Then *you* better learn to read it," said Justin. "Look." He pointed at the page. "That circle is an O. Say O."

"O," echoed Nicki.

"Once upon a time there was a worm . . ."

They didn't notice Gabby coast out of the yard on her bike.

Bucky jogged along beside her, taking long, bouncing steps. "What's your plan, Gab?"

"I'm going to find Miss Haliber's umbrella this afternoon," said Gabby. "That'll be easy. And then I'll have the rest of this week to work . . ." She slowed, dragging her foot, her eyes on something in Mr. Bashaw's yard. ". . . on the rest of my cases."

What was that, shining in the grass beside the Bashaws' house?

Dropping her bike, she went closer to investigate. Then she saw that it was only some flat pieces of tin. "Rats!" she muttered, turning back to the street, almost bumping into Bucky who had followed her.

"Huh?" he said, dancing out of her way.

"I thought that was one of the planting boxes," Gabby explained, picking up her bike. "But I guess it's just some metal Mr. Bashaw's using to fix his roof."

"I'm going to get my bike," said Bucky. "And my tape

recorder." He picked up speed, heading for home. "Don't do anything important until I get back," he called over his shoulder.

Gabby rode slowly. She was heading for the mall, but she might as well check out the neighborhood on the way. Was there a porch with some shiny new planting boxes on it? Did somebody's yard have a silver ball that hadn't been there yesterday?

Of course she was pretty sure people on Chilling Street wouldn't take stuff that didn't belong to them. But she had to be sure the missing things weren't somewhere nearby before she checked out other leads.

Bucky caught up with her. Gabby heard him talking into his tape recorder.

> "Ladies and Gentlemen, this is Tom Bucks on remote reporting from the scene of a bunch of weird crimes."

He went on talking, describing what she was doing.

Gabby turned onto Lillith Street, keeping her eyes open, circling and going back for a closer look at any yard where there was something suspicious. But the fact was, everything she wondered about turned out to have a perfectly sensible explanation.

She made a wide turn into the side gate at the mall and

pedaled along the backs of the stores. She locked her bike to the rack at the very end. The Lucky Ducky Supermarket was going to be her first stop.

Bucky poked his microphone at her. "Will you tell our audience whether you think the missing stuff might be here at the mall?"

"Well, not the garden things," Gabby mumbled into her coat front as she tugged her notebook and pencil out of her pocket.

"Speak up, please," Bucky said in his deep announcer's voice.

"Not the garden stuff," said Gabby, putting her mouth right up to the mike. "But Miss Haliber was in lots of the stores last week. Maybe she left her umbrella in one of them."

She pushed her way through a tangle of shopping carts blocking the door of the Lucky Ducky. The door whooshed open in front of her. Another sound slipped in and around the *whoosh* – music. Gabby backed up abruptly, bumping into Bucky again. That music – could it be –

"Hey, watch it!" Bucky complained. "Do you always have to smack into me like that?"

"Sorry," said Gabby. "But I just heard Hoot!" She darted around the corner. "He's back!" she crowed.

Parked in front of the Lucky Ducky was a white cart with square-dancing people painted on it. The music was guitar music, and the man playing it was wearing a white cowboy hat. Beside him sat his little black dog.

Hoot sold hot dogs and fruit squashes. He and his dog Annie were always the first sign of summer at the mall.

Gabby sorted out the money in her pocket. Yes, she had the price of a squash. She went to say hello to Hoot. He was the nicest man around the mall.

He squinted down at her. "Hello, there. Now, don't tell me, don't tell me . . . Gabby — that's it. How you doing, Gabby? My, you sure got tall since last summer."

She didn't even have to tell him what she wanted. He remembered. He handed her a raspberry squash.

"You, you're . . ." he said, lingering on the word, reaching into his cart while he looked at Bucky, "you're — Bucky. Right?" He gave Bucky a pineapple squash. "I'm not likely to forget that tape recorder. You taped Annie singing. I've still got that tape."

Bucky grinned. "I've got a copy, too. When I play it, our cat goes out of her mind."

Gabby sipped her squash. It was as sweet and good as she remembered from last summer.

"Ain't you hot in that outfit?" asked Hoot, eyeing her coat. "These are warm days."

Gabby shook her head. She looked down at Annie. "Annie's still wearing her little red coat. So I guess I can wear mine, too, if I want."

Hoot shook his head. "Different thing altogether. Annie's

getting on — she's almost fourteen now. That's ninety-eight people-years old. She's getting stiff and I keep her bundled up, cold days and warm. I even got her some boots to wear in the snow and rain."

"Boots!" exclaimed Gabby.

"You wear 'em, don't you?" asked Hoot.

Gabby admitted she did.

"Got to keep Annie's paws warm and dry," said Hoot. He strummed his guitar, tuning it, getting ready to sing.

"Hoot," Gabby said quickly, before he could start, "have you seen any funny-looking strangers around here?"

"Strangers!" snorted Hoot. "The world's nothing but strangers these days. Any special strangers you got in mind?"

"Crooks," said Gabby. "Will you tell me if you see someone like that?"

"You and the cops," Hoot assured her and began to sing about a letter edged in black. Annie put back her head and "sang" with him.

Gabby and Bucky dropped their squash cups in the trash basket outside the Lucky Ducky and went inside.

A lot of people were waiting to cash checks at the customer service desk and Gabby had to get into line.

"Bor-ing," said Bucky. "What can I say into my recorder about standing around in a line? Are we going to have to wait in lines every place you go?"

"You don't have to wait with me," said Gabby. "But I've

got to stay here. Maybe they've got the umbrella in their lost-and-found drawer."

The woman in charge was grumpy when Gabby finally got to the desk and asked about the umbrella. She poked around in a drawer. "Lost a roller skate? Or sunglasses? Or a library book?"

Gabby shook her head.

"Can't help you then, sis," said the woman. "Learn to hang onto your umbrellas."

"But it's not my — "

The woman didn't listen. She reached over Gabby's head and took a check from the man behind her.

Gabby crossed off the Lucky Ducky on the umbrella page in her book. She still had four other places to check out before dinner.

Bucky looked over her shoulder. "Why don't I go to a couple of those places and you go to the others. We'll save time."

Gabby's forehead puckered as she considered his offer. "But if you do that and you find the umbrella, then you're the private eye and I'm not."

Bucky thought for a minute. "Well, look at it this way. You're going to help me find my caiman, right? So, I sort of owe you."

And so Bucky checked out the Candle Light Candle Shoppe and the Pay Dirt, and Gabby asked about the umbrella in the Stitch in Time and the Card Shoppe. They met later at Hoot's cart. Gabby hadn't found the umbrella and neither had Bucky.

Gabby was surprised. There was nothing to finding a lost umbrella – right? Wrong! She hadn't found it. And now she was going to have to spend precious time hunting for it when she really needed the time to figure out who stole all the garden stuff.

She sighed. Well, she was a private eye, that's what counted. Problems just went with the territory.

7
Private Eye at Work

Usually Gabby liked Mondays. She had advanced math classes those days. And anyone who wanted to could spend the after-lunch period working with the word processors in the computer room. Yes. Monday was usually a pretty good day.

But this Monday draa-aaged. It was as slow as a snail crossing a sidewalk. Gabby thought the day would never end. All she wanted was to get on with her private-eye stuff. When the bell finally rang, she was the first one out of Mrs. Cole's classroom.

"No running in the halls," called a monitor as Gabby sped to the front doors.

She slowed down. But outside, she bounded down the steps.

"Wait for me," called Amy.

Gabby bounced up and down, running in place until Amy caught up with her. "I've got some goldfish," Amy panted.

"That's what my grandparents brought yesterday." Her eyes danced. She looked pleased.

"But I thought you didn't want goldfish," said Gabby. "I mean, you even said you can't hug a goldfish."

"Sure." Amy sighed. "But it's the best I can do this week. And anyway," she added cheerfully, "something's better than nothing."

"Maybe you'll get a real huggy pet yet," Gabby said encouragingly as they neared Amy's house.

Amy ran up the driveway. "I'll find you around after I get something to eat," she called.

Gabby entered her own house, running.

Fresh butterscotch cookies lay cooling on wax paper on the kitchen counter. She grabbed one in passing and bit into its salty-sweet goodness. Yum-my!

Mrs. O'Brien looked out of the laundry room. "Slow down." She snapped a towel briskly and folded it. "Whatever it is, it will wait a while longer."

But Gabby had had enough waiting.

She flew into her bedroom, dropped her book bag on the desk, and dug out her notebook and pencil. The den was her next stop. She took the big magnifying glass out of the desk and headed for the front hall to put on her private-eye coat.

She pawed through the coats in the closet, pushing them this way and that, rattling the hangers. Where was it? She shouldered her way past the coats and looked behind the folded-up card table. The private-eye coat wasn't there, either.

Mrs. O'Brien came through the hall carrying an armful of folded towels. "Are you looking for something?"

"My private-eye coat," Gabby explained. "I can't find it anywhere."

"Oh, I took winter things to the cleaners this morning," said Mrs. O'Brien, continuing on her way to the linen closet.

Gabby followed her, horrified. "We've got to get it back," she said desperately. "I'm going out to do my private-eye stuff, and I really need it. Can I call the cleaners?"

Mrs. O'Brien was calm. "It's much too warm to wear that coat now. And it's too late to get it back. It's probably already dunked in cleaning solution."

"I won't look like a private eye," Gabby moaned. "How can I be a private eye if I don't look like one?"

"Make believe you're wearing it. You used to be pretty good at make-believe." Mrs. O'Brien actually sounded cheerful.

Gabby scowled and stomped to the kitchen for another cookie.

"I'll be out for a while," called Mrs. O'Brien, "picking up Nicole at little Bess's birthday party. Remember: Don't go out of the neighborhood."

Gabby slammed the back door and headed for the Oakleys', chomping on her cookie. How could your very own mother be so unfeeling! Didn't she know that part of being a private eye was looking like one? It was called having . . . having . . . an *image*. People believed you if you looked like what you were supposed to be.

Bluff was chained on the porch. When he saw Gabby he wagged his tail so hard it beat like a drum on the porch floor. His mouth open, he seemed to be smiling at her.

Gabby stopped to give him a good roughing up. "Is Mr. Oakley gone, Bluff?" she asked, holding his face between her hands and looking into his eyes. "Are you being a tough watchdog? Hm? But that's silly. You aren't tough. You're just a big bluffer. You wouldn't hurt a flea."

"Awwwwrr-rr," said Bluff, wriggling and licking her chin.

She hugged him. "Now don't you go barking at me, Bluff. I'm going to look around the yard for clues."

She went to the bush beside the steps, the one with the missing lights. Dropping to her knees, she inspected the ground around it, using her magnifying glass.

"The birds have come back from the south," said Amy, coming up behind her. "They're all over the yard. Hey, what are you doing?"

"Looking for footprints," said Gabby, her eyes on the ground. "And for broken pieces from this bush." At last she got up and stuffed the magnifying glass into her belt.

"Well?" asked Amy. "Are there any?"

"Nope," said Gabby. She stood on tiptoe and touched the top of the bush, measuring how tall it was.

"Now what?" demanded Amy. "Hey, let me look at your magnifying glass." She took it out of Gabby's belt and held it up to one eye. The eye became enormous.

Gabby didn't want to play games. "This bush is taller than I am," she explained. "So that means the crook is at least as tall as I am, maybe taller." A bit of color on one of the branches near the back of the bush caught her eye.

"Hey, I need my glass," she said, taking it from Amy. She held it near the bush. A tangle of threads was caught there. A clue! The crook had caught his clothes on the bush. She picked up the threads with two fingers and placed them carefully between the pages of her notebook.

"I guess those are from the crook's clothes, huh?" said Amy.

"Could be," said Gabby, writing in her book: Threads. Maybe from crook's shirt.

With Bluff looking forlornly after them, Gabby and Amy headed for the McCabes'. Maybe that crook had left a clue, too.

The porch was empty. The two planting boxes that had been there yesterday were gone. Had the crook come back for them? Gabby's heart skipped. It would be neat to catch him red-handed.

Silently she tiptoed from one side of the house to the

other, peering around the corners to see if someone was hiding.

Amy, her eyes like circles, tiptoed after Gabby. "What are you looking for?" she whispered.

Gabby held a finger to her lips and Amy was quiet.

There was nobody in either of the side yards. Her back against the wall, Gabby inched along the side of the house and peeked into the backyard. She let out her breath in disappointment. Nobody was there. Rats!

"I thought the crook might be here," she explained to Amy. "But there's nobody around now."

"What would you have done if he was here?" Amy asked curiously.

Gabby thought about that. But she knew what she would have done, anyway. "Made a citizen's arrest," she said.

The planting boxes weren't sitting inside the garage, nor were they next to the trash cans beside the garage. As Gabby moved into the open, sunlight glinted off something on the patio. She went near.

Two of the green wooden boxes on the brick floor were filled with pink geraniums. The other two were empty. Shiny metal showed around the rims of the green flower-filled boxes. The geraniums were planted in the metal boxes, and the metal boxes nestled inside the fancy green ones.

A window swung open above them and Mrs. McCabe

leaned out. "Aren't they pretty?" she called. "I filled the two liners this morning. Of course," she chattered on, "the patio is out of balance now, with just two of the boxes planted. I do hope you'll find the other boxes soon, dear."

"Yes, ma'am," said Gabby. "I hope so, too." Then she corrected herself. "I mean, you just bet I'll find them soon."

She led the way back to the front porch and examined it with great care. There were no dusty footprints, no scratches on the paint, no threads caught in any cracks

She sat on the steps and on the McCabe page in her notebook wrote: No clues.

Amy perched on the railing, swinging her feet. "I guess if I was a crook, I wouldn't want you coming after me," she said.

Gabby didn't look up. She read what she had written. Then, biting her lip, thinking, she added something more: Maybe there's a clue here and I'm just not seeing it. Come back tomorrow and look again.

Without any clues, the McCabe case was going to be hard to crack.

"You know," said Amy, jumping off the railing and following Gabby to Mrs. Driscoll's house, "it's neat the way you write stuff in your book. Are you going to show it to everyone on Career Day?"

Gabby hadn't thought about that. But her notebook would be good to show. It had the drawing of the umbrella in it, and the stores she had visited were checked off. It had her thoughts about the crimes. It even had a clue, the threads. By Friday it would be filled with notes and clues. It would be great to show at school – along with telling everybody the answers to the mysteries.

There weren't any footprints to look at in Mrs. Driscoll's garden. If only Gabby had stopped Mrs. Driscoll from planting those pansies! But she hadn't thought about it then. And now the ground around the pillar was neatly dug up and raked and filled with the flowers.

Amy leaned forward and with a finger traced the words on a metal plate on the rim of the pillar. "First Place Gracious Garden Designs," she read. "Golly. I'd feel terrible too if everyone told me I did something wonderful and then somebody stole my prize." She turned to Gabby. "How do you suppose the silver ball stayed stuck on here?"

Gabby smoothed a hand across the top of the pillar. It felt like a saucer. "The ball sort of fitted into this place," she explained. "It couldn't roll off."

"It wasn't glued down or something?" asked Amy. "It just sat there?"

"It just sat there," Gabby agreed. Anybody who could lift it had been able to carry away the silver ball.

That made her wonder. How heavy was the ball? She began writing furiously: Does the ball weigh a hundred pounds? Does it take a really strong person to lift it?

She stared at the pillar absent-mindedly, biting on her pencil. Where had she seen strong people lately? A thought tickled the back of her mind. Then it popped to the surface. She wrote: Check out the health club. Lots of strong-looking guys went into the health club at the mall.

"I guess it's going to be hard solving the crimes, Gab," said Amy as they followed the path past the troll sign and the bridge and the bushes shaped like animals. "I mean," she added as they turned onto the street, "the only clue you've got are those threads." She looked worried.

"I've still got three days to do it," said Gabby. Maybe being a private eye was going to be harder than she had thought. But still – three whole days was lots of time.

8

Ruined!

Gabby finished putting the forks and spoons in their tray and closed the drawer. She gathered up the cooking pans and stacked them in the low cabinet next to the stove. There. Her after-dinner job was done.

"Can I go now, Mom?" she asked.

Mrs. O'Brien looked around the neat kitchen. She flipped a dish towel over her shoulder and smiled. "You're getting to be a real help, honey. I don't even have to tell you how to do things anymore."

Gabby didn't exactly enjoy after-dinner chores. But she did have to admit she liked the grown-up feeling she had when she and Mom worked together in the kitchen.

"Toddle off," said Mrs. O'Brien.

Gabby headed down the hall, forgetting about spoons and cooking pans. She came to a dead stop in the doorway of the bedroom, frozen, her eyes fastened on Nicki. "My notebook!" she yelped as she took in what Nicki was doing. "What are you doing to my notebook!"

Nicki was lying on the floor. Coloring books and crayons were scattered around her. But she wasn't coloring in any coloring book. She looked up over her shoulder at Gabby. "Making it pretty," she said, lifting her hand from the page. "See?"

Nicki said it sweetly. But she looked guilty even as she spoke. The page with the drawing of Miss Haliber's umbrella was scribbled red and purple.

Gabby dived for the notebook. "You're not supposed to touch that," she wailed. "It was on the desk on my side of the room. It's got all my private-eye stuff in it."

Nicki scrambled toward the door, holding the book out of reach. "I'm not finished," she yelled.

"Oh . . . yes . . . you . . . are!" said Gabby, trying to catch her.

Mrs. O'Brien appeared in the hall. She caught Nicki's outstretched arm. "What's going on here?"

"My notebook," said Gabby. "Nicki . . ." Her voice shook. "She's . . ." She couldn't finish.

Mrs. O'Brien pried the notebook out of Nicki's hand and gave it to Gabby. "Nicole, you know you are not to touch the things on Gabrielle's desk."

Nicki's lower lip pushed out. "I was helping Gabby," she said, putting on her best baby act.

Mrs. O'Brien didn't give in. "Nicole, you know you're in the wrong. Apologize to your sister."

Tears spilled down Nicki's cheeks. She looked up pitifully at Mrs. O'Brien. "I'm just the baby of the family," she lisped.

Mrs. O'Brien was firm. "Even babies must apologize sometimes. What do you say to Gabrielle?"

"I — " Nicki hiccupped. "I'm sorry." With her wet face, she really did look sorry. But it was hard to tell the difference between sorry and not-sorry when Nicki pulled her baby-of-the-family act.

Gabby had been looking through her notebook. Green scribbles marked some of the pages. The umbrella was ruined. What was she going to do about it!

She heard her mother's voice. "Gabrielle, what do you say?"

Gabby took a deep breath. It sure was hard to forgive Nicki when she acted like a monster. But Mom and Dad said forgiveness was part of being a decent person. She let out her breath. "It's okay, Nicki."

"Tub time," said Mrs. O'Brien, hustling Nicki toward the bathroom. As she passed, she gave Gabby a quick hug. "Tom," she called, lifting her voice, "our older daughter needs moral support."

Mr. O'Brien's voice came from the living room. "Hey, Number-One-Daughter. Come see your old dad."

Gabby trailed into the living room. Her great notebook was ruined. She held it out, opened to the umbrella page. "I need this drawing to recognize Miss Haliber's umbrella when I find it." She couldn't help it — her voice shook.

"So." Mr. O'Brien took the book, looking closely at the pages. "The phantom struck again, eh?" He took a pen out of his shirt pocket and flipped through the notebook to an empty page. "Let's see what kind of an artist I am."

With quick, short strokes, he began to sketch another umbrella. He kept turning the pages back to the Miss Haliber–Nicki artwork.

Gabby leaned on his shoulder. "It's got a tassel exactly like that one," she said, pointing to Miss Haliber's drawing.

"Tassel coming up," said Mr. O'Brien, studying the drawing under the red and purple smudges and adding to his sketch. "Nicki seems to be giving you a hard time these days," he said, his eyes on his drawing.

"She's a pain," said Gabby. "Remember how great it used to be when she was little and cute? She's really terrible now."

"All the time?" The umbrella was getting better by the minute. "Think about it. Is she terrible all of the time?"

"Welllll. . ." Gabby thought. "Sometimes she's still okay."

Mr. O'Brien held the drawing away and squinted at it. "How's that?"

Gabby squinted, too. "It's almost as good as Miss Haliber's drawing," she said. "You know, she said the umbrella got rained on in London and Paris and that's why she likes it."

Mr. O'Brien took the notebook out of her hand. He added some slanting lines. "Paris rain," he said. He drew a puddle with splashing raindrops under the umbrella. "London puddle."

Gabby giggled. Then she turned serious. "We're spoiling Nicki, Daddy," she said. "She does bratty things and says it's okay because she's the baby of the family."

Mr. O'Brien nodded. "I think our baby is about to find out that growing up can be tough."

Gabby was suddenly alarmed. "You're not going to spank her!"

Mr. O'Brien shook his head. "But Nicki's old enough to understand that she's got to play by the rules." He reached out and mussed Gabby's hair. "Don't worry about it. Mom and I are going to start working on Nicki's character. She'll turn out to be as nice as you are."

He closed the notebook and handed it to her. "How's the gumshoe business coming along?"

"Well" – Gabby hated to admit it – "it's harder to catch crooks than I thought."

"MMM-mm," said Mr. O'Brien, settling back in his chair. "Wily characters, crooks. Never do what you expect them to."

"But I've got one clue," said Gabby, brightening. "I found some threads on one of Mr. Oakley's bushes. I think the crook caught his sleeve or something."

"Sounds like a promising lead," said Mr. O'Brien.

"Somehow I get the feeling you're going to crack your cases. Now, let me make a suggestion. If one of your crooks needs a mouthpiece, tell him to call your old dad. That's known as keeping business in the family. And — who knows? — I just might be able to help him stay out of the slammer."

"But not if he really did the crime," Gabby said sternly.

"Not if you catch him red-handed." Mr. O'Brien laughed. "Do that and we'll lock him up. And I'll see to it that you personally get to throw away the key."

9

A Clue for the Birds

"**H**ey, Gab."

The voice came from behind her. Gabby was sitting cross-legged on the floor of the Learning Media Center. Everyone was there. They were listening to Miss Held, the school nurse, talk about careers in health. She was pointing to a skeleton and telling how bones and muscles work together so people can walk and move their arms. It was all part of Career Week.

"Hey, Gabby O'."

Gabby didn't turn around. She knew who was sitting behind her.

"That bunch of bones – that's you with no skin on," Justin hissed.

Gabby acted as though she didn't hear him. No way was she going to give Justin a chance to Gotcha! her.

"That skeleton used to be alive," Justin whispered.

The hair on the back of Gabby's neck moved from Justin's breath. She shook her head to get rid of his breath in her hair and try to make him move away from her. He was too close.

"Only now it's" — he whispered the word hoarsely — "deeaaad." He began to sing softly. "Oh, the worms crawl in, the worms crawl out, and you don't know what it's all about."

Gabby swung around, bumping into him. "Justin, you are simply too gross."

"Gotcha!" Justin doubled over, laughing. "Gotcha!" he gasped.

Gabby leaned her forehead on her knee. Caught again. How could Justin be so awful to her and so nice to Nicki!

"You are weird, Justin," she said wearily as they got up to go back to their classroom. "Wacko weird."

Back in class, Mrs. Cole talked about some of the other people who would be visiting. "Tomorrow we'll hear about law enforcement, and — "

Gabby's ears perked up. Was a real private eye maybe going to come to school?

" — later in the week a photographer will be here. So will a newspaper editor. The engineer who designed the new Fifth Street bridge — "

"What about an inventor. Are we going to hear an inventor?"

Everybody swung around in their seats and stared. Porter had come out of his usually dreamy state. He had actually asked a question. Porter hardly ever asked questions.

Mrs. Cole seemed surprised, too. "Why, I'm not sure, Porter. It might be hard to find an inventor. That's not a common career."

"Oh." Porter lost interest. He began to draw something in his notebook.

Mrs. Cole tried to get his attention back. "Porter . . ." she said. "Porter?"

Porter looked up.

"I'll talk to our careers coordinator," Mrs. Cole said hastily. "We'll see if he can find an inventor.

"Now, people – " She clapped her hands. Everyone had started to talk. "I hope you're thinking about your own careers. I hope you're researching them. Remember what we've learned about the use of the computer catalog and – "

Gabby stroked her notebook. It looked pretty good, with the new drawing of the umbrella and the pages she had rewritten to replace the ones Nicki had ruined. She could even show her first clue.

She opened the book to the page where she had taped the threads. They had to have come from the crook's sleeve because they had been caught quite high up on the bush. One of the threads was thin and pink, another was thick and green, and the third was long and sort of tan. That had to be a funny-looking shirt!

She closed the notebook, a nagging thought tugging at her mind. It was Tuesday. She only had two-and-a-half more days to work on the crimes. She needed something more than a couple of threads. She needed a strong lead. Maybe she wouldn't —

"Stop that!" she said to herself. "You just stop that! Don't think about not being able to solve the crimes. Think about how you *are* going to do it."

She was going to talk to Mrs. Driscoll today about how heavy the silver ball was. And she was going to look up the addresses of fortunetellers in the phone book.

She was proud of that idea. Who used shiny silver balls? Fortunetellers, that's who! The thought had come to her as she drifted off to sleep last night. Maybe a fortuneteller had taken the silver ball. Maybe a fortuneteller was looking into it this very minute, telling somebody what lay in their future.

She looked at the things she had written last night:

Here is what I think:

All the crooks came early in the morning.
Mr. Oakley's crook is tall enough to take the lights off the top of the bush.
Maybe he wore a pink and green and tan shirt.
Nobody saw the crooks.
Did they see each other?
Did they know each other?

The notes added up to something. Early morning plus

crooks maybe seeing each other equaled — what? "A gang!" she thought. Maybe there weren't three separate crooks. Maybe they were all in it together — a gang!

Quickly she added *a gang* to her list.

But — what would a gang do with all that strange stuff? Did they sell it? Who'd want to buy it! One answer just seemed to lead to another question.

The caiman. Gabby remembered Bucky's caiman as she was walking home from school. Bucky had already helped her look for the umbrella and she owed him. She turned in at the Bucks' walk.

Bucky's mother answered the door when Gabby rang. "Bucky isn't here, Gabrielle. You can find him at baseball practice."

Gabby knew that. "I wanted to ask you about Bucky's caiman," she said.

Mrs. Bucks shuddered.

"I guess you haven't found it yet," said Gabby.

Mrs. Bucks made a face. "You guessed right. If somebody doesn't find it soon, I'm going to have a breakdown."

Gabby explained about her promise to Bucky and Mrs. Bucks swung the door wide. "Be my guest."

Gabby went indoors. With Mrs. Bucks following, she looked everywhere, starting with the refrigerator. The caiman wasn't under it, or under the kitchen sink, or behind the stove. It wasn't under any of the beds or behind the draperies or among the plants on the dining-room window sill.

Gabby tried to think where she would hide if she were a caiman. She looked in the shower and in Bucky's closet, which was a worse mess than hers.

Bucky's sister's bedroom door was closed. She opened it a crack when Gabby knocked.

"It can't be in here," said Laurie. "I've kept my door locked ever since that creature got out of its cage."

And so that was that.

Gabby said thank you and she guessed that was all for now and went outside. She sat on the front steps and listed all the places she had looked. And she thought. She couldn't help thinking. She couldn't find a little old lost caiman. She couldn't even find an umbrella.

Sighing, she closed her notebook and went to see Mrs. Driscoll to ask whether the shiny ball was solid silver.

"Oh, but it isn't silver at all!" exclaimed Mrs. Driscoll. "It has quicksilver – mercury – in it. That's what makes it like a mirror."

Gabby was disappointed. "Then it's not worth a whole lot of money?"

"My dear!" Mrs. Driscoll sounded sorry for Gabby. "It's a thing of beauty, and you can't put a dollar value on beauty."

Not worth lots of money Gabby wrote in her book. She

went on to her next question. "Does it weigh tons and tons?"

Mrs. Driscoll brushed dirt off a pansy face. "Not awfully. It's not too heavy for me to carry, so I suppose the thief could carry it."

So. She didn't have to hang around the health club looking for big muscles after all. Gabby crossed that idea off her list.

"I'm glad you're working so hard on this, Gabrielle." Mrs. Driscoll ran a finger over the words on the rim of the pillar. "I just hope you find the globe before the garden walk on Saturday," she added wistfully.

Gabby trudged home, thinking. If the crook hadn't taken the silver ball to get rich, why had he taken it? Because he liked to look at himself in it and see his nose get all big and huge? The thought made her grin. But then she kicked at a stone and watched it bounce ahead of her down the sidewalk. She wasn't getting anywhere at all with these crimes.

Mr. Oakley leaned on his rake, watching her. "Any luck, sis?" he asked as she came near.

Gabby shook her head. She hated having to admit she hadn't yet found the lights. But the truth was she hadn't, and that was that.

Mr. Oakley sat on the porch steps and lit his pipe. "Well," he said, squinting at her through a cloud of sweet-smelling smoke, "I can't wait forever." He tapped a garden catalog that lay on the steps. "I better send away for new bulbs. If I don't, I won't be able to light up the yard for Memorial Day."

Gabby dropped onto the step beside him. Her elbows on her knees, she cradled her chin in her hands, watching a robin flutter around the lawn. "Please give me a couple more days."

"Well . . ."

"I just know I'll find them," said Gabby. Inside, the small voice whispered, Maybe you won't. Maybe — "Stop it!" she said to herself.

Mr. Oakley directed a sharp look at her. "Now, sis," he said, "don't you feel bad if you don't find the lights. It's expecting a lot of a kid your age. Matter of fact, I've begun to think I was too hard on you. I'll pay you in full, find them or not."

Gabby's chin poked forward. Mr. Oakley was nice, even though he was gruff. But a deal was a deal. You didn't go back on a handshake. "I'll find 'em," she vowed. "See if I don't."

Mr. Oakley changed the subject. "Something nice is happening around here. Someone's moving in."

Gabby leaned forward, looking at the empty house across the street. "You mean on the corner?"

"Shh. Don't make any sudden movements." Mr. Oakley pointed. "See that bird? She doesn't want us around here."

Only then did Gabby really see the robin that fluttered nearby. It had been there for some time.

"Check out the bush behind us," Mr. Oakley said in a low voice.

Gabby twisted around. At the back of the bush was a tangle of threads and dried grass. "A nest!" she breathed softly. "That robin's building a nest."

"Nest means eggs." Mr. Oakley tapped his pipe on the side of the steps. "And eggs mean baby birds. That ma bird is going to tell off anyone who goes near that bush for the next few weeks."

"What'll you do?" asked Gabby.

"Keep Bluff out of the front yard for a while," said Mr. Oakley. "And it looks like we won't be using our front door until the Fourth of July."

Suddenly Gabby remembered her clue. She opened her book and looked at the tangle of threads. Her heart did a nose dive. The threads weren't a clue at all! She had found them in the very place where the robin was building the nest.

She pulled the threads away from the tape and let them sail away on the breeze. The tangle floated to the grass. Even as Gabby watched, the robin swooped low and picked it up.

And now Gabby was right back where she had started, with no clues. Not a single one.

She remembered something else. "So now Bluff can't be a watchdog, either. And maybe the crook will come back and take the rest of the lights."

She and Mr. Oakley stared at each other.

"And he'll scare the robin and her babies," Gabby said sadly. And that seemed even worse than taking some more of Mr. Oakley's lights.

At home, she dragged the telephone yellow-page book out of its drawer. She sat on the floor and, turning to *F,* ran a finger down the pages, reading. Flowers. Fly Spray. Food, Carry Out. Food, Cat and Dog. Formal Wear. Fossil Rocks. . . .

Her lips moving, she said the alphabet to herself. " . . . *o* . . . *p* . . . *q* . . . *r* . . *s* . . . *t* . . . " Fortuneteller should have been between Formal Wear and Fossil Rocks. There weren't any fortunetellers in the phone book.

She went to her room, thinking about clues — and not having any — and gangs — and if there was one, how she could find out about it.

She curled up on her bed, looking at all the ideas in her book. They were good ideas. And not one of them had led her anywhere.

Well. She sighed. She still had two days to work on her cases. Two whole days.

But — would that be enough time?

10

Feeling Miserable

"No," said Mrs. O'Brien, "you may not be excused from Brownie meeting. I'm your leader and the meeting is at our house. How would it look if you weren't here?"

It was the next morning. Mrs. O'Brien was playing Tough Mother today.

"But I don't have much time left before Friday," Gabby pleaded. "There's still stuff I need to do after school if I'm going to solve the crimes."

"No," said Mrs. O'Brien.

"And if I don't solve them, Justin will say I couldn't and he'll say Gotcha!"

Nicki looked up from her bowl of Choconuts. "Justin reads to me. I love him."

Gabby shuddered and pretended not to hear. "I promised I'd find the missing stuff, Mom. You wouldn't want me to back out of a promise, would you?"

"The meeting will be short," Mrs. O'Brien said serenely.

"You'll have time afterward to track down criminals."

"You're ruining my life," moaned Gabby.

"You can save time by putting on your Brownie uniform this morning," said Mrs. O'Brien. "We'll start promptly after school. Now finish your milk and scoot, or you'll be late."

Gabby gulped her milk and dashed.

Her mother's voice followed her. "And don't forget that we're having your teeth checked after school tomorrow."

Gabby had forgotten. She groaned. Dr. Payne was very nice, even though he had such a terrible name. Only she didn't want to see him this week. Everything this week was getting in the way of her private-eye work.

And school was just as bad as home. Mrs. Cole kept them busy every single minute. Gabby hardly had time even to peek into her notebook and think about things.

In the middle of science class, the fire alarm rang. Porter was just telling them how he had tried making plastic for one of his space models by pouring some chemicals on cold water in the bathtub. The stuff was supposed to harden on top of the water and he could just pick it up. Right in the middle of what he was saying, they all had to go to the nearest exit without running and wait outside school until it was okay to go back in the building.

They hopped around in line outdoors, waiting, and Porter said his experiment hadn't worked. He couldn't get the goop off the bathtub. Now everybody in his family had to shower in the basement. He was going to have to figure out a way to wash away the mess.

They all kept looking for smoke and listening for fire engines. But there wasn't a fire after all. A fire would have been exciting, Gabby thought. Going outside was just a practice drill.

No sooner had they gone back indoors than the lunch bell rang. Mrs. Cole looked desperate and said, "Mercy, when are we going to have some quiet time for just plain learning!"

Gabby and Amy and Bucky and Justin and Porter sat together in the lunch room.

Amy dribbled ketchup in little plops onto her hot dog. "Bucky," she asked, "did you look under your refrigerator? Did you find your caiman?"

Bucky shook his head. "Nope."

"Nope didn't find it or nope didn't look?" demanded Amy.

"Looked," said Bucky. "Didn't find it. Gabby looked too." He bit into his hot dog. "My mom thought she stepped on it last night. The hall was dark and she was barefoot. She screeched so loud she woke everybody up. Only it wasn't the caiman – she just stepped on my baseball glove."

Amy pushed away her plate. "Your caiman must be hungry and I can't eat. Bucky, you ought to put some food where he'll find it."

That gave Gabby an idea. "Bucky," she said slowly, thinking, "if you put food in a couple of places . . . and then some of it's gone from just one place . . . you'll know where to look for the caiman."

Bucky stopped in midbite. "Hey, that's really smart, Gab."

"And the caiman won't be hungry anymore," said Amy, "even if you don't find him." She began to smile and reached for her plate. "Maybe I can eat a little bit after all."

"Have you found any of the missing stuff, Gab?" asked Justin.

Gabby eyed him suspiciously. Was Justin setting her up again? But Justin sat there looking like a perfectly normal person. He didn't have his demon look.

She hated to admit she hadn't solved the mysteries yet. But she told the truth. "Mrs. Driscoll is really sad," she said. "I think she cries. Mr. Oakley says he won't turn on the lights in his yard till he gets some more to match the ones that are there. He's going to have to order them from New York." She finished by telling how there were no fortune-tellers in town and the silver ball wasn't real, true silver.

"I've got an idea," said Justin. "Sometimes the big kids have scavenger hunts. Maybe they took that stuff."

"What's a scavenger hunt?" Amy wanted to know.

"The kids get lists of weird stuff they're supposed to find

and take back to a party," Justin explained. "The ones who get the most things on their list get a prize."

Gabby looked closely at Justin. Why was he all of a sudden being nice? But she was willing to follow any lead. "Was there a scavenger hunt?" she asked.

Justin shrugged. "Don't know. But the stuff was missing Sunday. People go to parties on Saturday night. So?"

The scavenger hunt was a pretty good lead, and Gabby got excited again about maybe solving the mysteries. But before she could do anything about it, she had to get through the rest of the school day and Brownie meeting.

They were doing art projects in Brownies. Gabby finished her juice-can penguin, and then she helped Sally. If she hadn't, Brownie meeting would have gone on all night. Sally was making a mobile. It all hung down on one side, and Gabby helped her make it hang right. Then they both helped Barbie blow on the paint on her memory rock. But the paint wouldn't dry, even with three people whooshing at it.

At last Mrs. O'Brien said Barbie could leave the rock to dry until next week. And then Brownie meeting was over.

Gabby was the first one out the door.

"Gabrielle, say good-bye to your guests," called her mother.

But Gabby didn't have time. She had to talk to all the big kids she could find before dinner.

Laurie Bucks came to the door holding her fingers out

stiffly to let her nail polish dry. "A scavenger hunt? Oh, no," she said positively, "there couldn't have been one. I would have been asked."

The Clifton twins were digging around the birch tree in their yard.

"Be sure to dig deep enough for the water to get down to the roots," their mother called from the front door.

The twins didn't know about any scavenger hunts, either.

"Sure sounds like fun, though," said Chad.

"Let's get one together," said Charlie.

Gabby talked to every big kid she met on her way to the mall. She even talked with the boys who bagged groceries in the Lucky Ducky. Nobody knew anything about a scavenger hunt.

She slumped against the railing outside the Duck, glumly watching the doors swing open like magic every time someone came near. Career Day was the day after tomorrow. She wasn't going to be able to tell firsthand how private eyes work. All she could do was show her dumb old ad and her dumb old notebook and tell how she had failed.

She hadn't found any of the missing things, let alone caught the crooks who took them. She hadn't even been able to find a lost umbrella when she knew where it had to be. She had gone not only to the stores Miss Haliber told her about, but to the bookmobile as well. And she had read all the lost-and-found ads in the paper.

Something soft and warm brushed against her ankle.

Gabby looked down into Annie's wise, old eyes. Annie whimpered softly.

Gabby scooped her up. "Hi, pup," she whispered. "You came to make me feel better, didn't you."

Annie's feathery tail waved like a small flag.

Gabby stood there feeling miserable, cuddling Annie, wondering why she had ever thought she could be a private eye.

11

A Real No-Mistake Clue

The next day in school was as bad as any day could be. Mrs. Cole made them all do extra math problems because so many people were having trouble with fractions. And she said nobody could use calculators. There was a hot dish for lunch with everything mushed together so you couldn't tell what was in it. Gabby deeply distrusted hot dishes. And Justin said Gotcha! three times – the last time just before Mrs. O'Brien came to pick up Gabby early to go to see Dr. Payne.

Gabby hopped into the car and banged the door shut and bounced on the seat and said, "I hate Justin Abrams."

"I don't hate Justin," said Nicki. She was sitting in the back seat wearing her Kitty Nose. The whiskers wobbled when she talked.

Mrs. O'Brien drove away slowly from school. "Now, why would you hate a nice boy like Justin?"

"Because he says things and when I believe him he says

Gotcha!" said Gabby. "He said nobody fed the fish in our tank. So when I went and asked Mrs. Cole for the fish food, she said Tommy Riccio fed them and when I went back to the reading corner Justin laughed like crazy and said 'Gotcha!' I hate Justin."

Mrs. O'Brien looked at her sideways as they stopped at a traffic light. "It sounds to me as though Justin likes you."

"Likes me!" groaned Gabby. Her mother had awfully weird ideas about liking!

"Sometimes boys tease the girls they like," said Mrs. O'Brien.

"Justin can't like Gabby," piped the voice from the back seat. "He reads to me. I'm going to marry Justin."

"Mom!" hissed Gabby. "Stop her! What if she says that to him!"

"He'd know it's a sweet compliment from a very little girl," said Mrs. O'Brien, turning into the parking lot at the dental clinic. "When Justin teases you, he's just trying to make you notice him."

"I notice him all right," Gabby said darkly.

Mrs. O'Brien eased into an empty parking space. "Look at Justin's teasing the right way. I'm serious about his probably liking you."

"Don't say that in front of Nicki," Gabby whispered hoarsely. "She might tell the kids. I'd die!" She slid down in the seat. "I would ab-so-lutely die."

"We'll talk about it tonight," Mrs. O'Brien said in a low voice.

Dr. Payne poked around in her mouth and said "No Cavities" and she didn't need braces yet. Yet. That meant she was going to need them, and Gabby only half minded. All the older girls at school had braces on their teeth. She felt almost grown-up as they left Dr. Payne's office.

Mrs. O'Brien let her out of the car at the corner of Chilling Street and went on home. Gabby stood there for a minute, fingering her notebook, deciding what to do next. Maybe she wasn't going to solve the mysteries. But she wasn't going to stop trying until there wasn't a shred of hope left. She wouldn't give up. She wasn't a quitter. She —

Yip. Yip-yip.

Gabby came out of her thoughts.

The house on the corner was no longer empty. Curtains hung at the windows and white wicker chairs stood on the porch. An old lady was sitting in one of the chairs holding a small black poodle. It barked again, and the woman smiled at Gabby.

Gabby smiled back and started up the walk to say hello.

"Gab-ree-elle? Gab-ree-elle?"

Her name floated through the neighborhood.

Gabby stopped and looked around.

"Yoo-hoo. Here, dear." Mrs. Driscoll was waving at her from beside a sitting-up-bear bush. "I must see you," she called.

Gabby ran across the street.

Mrs. Driscoll put her big garden scissors down on the grass and dug into her pocket. She handed Gabby a folded piece of paper.

Puzzled, Gabby opened it.

The note didn't have an opening. It didn't say "Dear Mrs. Driscoll." And it wasn't signed. All it said was:

Garden ball ok. Do not worry.

A clue! A real, no-mistake clue! "Where did you get this?" Gabby asked breathlessly. "When?"

"It was in my mailbox with the other mail," said Mrs. Driscoll.

"Have you got the envelope? Where was it mailed from. Maybe we can tell from — "

"Oh, but it wasn't mailed," said Mrs. Driscoll, picking up the big scissors. "It was there, just like that, without an envelope. Why, it doesn't even have my name on it!"

Gabby's mind raced, adding up ideas. She studied the note closely. The words weren't cut out of a newspaper or magazine and pasted onto the paper the way ransom notes always were. And they weren't printed or written with a pen, either.

"It's typewritten," murmured Mrs. Driscoll.

"Did the McCabes and the Oakleys get notes?" demanded Gabby.

"Why, I never thought to ask," said Mrs. Driscoll. "Ben Oakley has been away today. But I think Claire McCabe is at home."

All of Gabby's discouragement was forgotten. "This is a great clue. I'll need it for a while." She folded the paper and slipped it into her pocket. "Don't worry," she called over her shoulder as she headed for the McCabes'. "I think I'm going to find the silver ball."

The kitchen lights were on. Gabby went to the side entrance and rang the bell. Mrs. McCabe came to the door. Her hands were white with flour and she held them up the way doctors on TV do after they've washed their hands.

"Oh, Gabrielle," she said, "I'm glad to see you. I found something in our mailbox today. You'll want to see it." With a floury finger she pointed at her apron pocket. "Reach into my pocket. There's a piece of paper there."

Gabby's heart was thudding. At last! The case was breaking.

The note said:

Planting boxes ok. Do not worry.

The note was just like Mrs. Driscoll's, without a Dear Somebody or a Yours Truly.

"This wasn't in an envelope, right?" Gabby asked, looking up at Mrs. McCabe.

"Why, no it wasn't," said Mrs. McCabe. "But how did you know?"

Gabby was already running toward the Oakleys'. "I'll tell you pretty soon," she called. She turned and ran backwards, laughing. "I think I'm going to find your planting boxes, Mrs. McCabe."

She knew what she was going to find at the Oakleys', and find it she did. Mr. Oakley had just come home. He was standing at the mailbox when Gabby got there.

The note was like the others:

Lights ok. Do not worry.

She ran home and spread the notes out side by side on the desk in the den. Then she turned the lamp up to Bright, got out the magnifying glass, and studied the words on the notes.

"Uh-*huh*," she murmured, grinning. "Yep." And, finally, "All *right*!"

12

The Mystery of the Missing Stuff

Gabby laid out her clothes before she went to bed. She put things where she could find them easily in the morning. She even tucked clean socks into her shoes so she wouldn't have to rummage around, making noise.

She had a small alarm clock that looked like a golf ball. She set it for five o'clock and tucked it under her pillow. Nicki wouldn't hear it when it rang and wake up when she got up.

Turning off the lamp, she slid into bed. Then she lay with her arms under her head, staring up at the glow-in-the-dark stars on the ceiling.

Tomorrow was Career Day. Maybe, just maybe, she was going to have the mystery of the missing stuff solved after all. *If* she found what she expected to find in the morning.

Ideas danced in her head like bobbing butterflies. Notes that all said practically the same thing . . . notes printed on the same kind of paper . . . the letters in the printing all exactly alike . . . notes that had not been mailed . . . notes with wings. . . . Her eyelids drooped.

She dreamed a shiny planting box flew overhead. Nicki was in it, waving. Mrs. Driscoll was having a garage sale. Every time she sold something, big tears slid down her cheeks and plopped onto a troll standing at her feet. The troll had a great, huge nose and his mouth and eyes slanted back from his nose as though he had looked at himself in the silver ball and stayed that way forever. Justin doubled over laughing. "Gotcha! Gotcha!" Amy walked past, leading a lion on a red leash. Porter came along pulling a grandfather clock in a yellow wagon. The clock announced the hour. Bong . . . bing . . . ting-ting-ting –

Gabby's eyes popped open. She reached under her pillow and turned off the alarm clock. Quickly she looked across the room at Nicki.

Nicki twisted and turned and faced Gabby. But her eyes stayed closed.

Silently, Gabby slipped out of bed and pulled on her clothes. She tiptoed out of the room, carrying her shoes.

She grabbed her jacket and let herself out the kitchen door and sat on the steps to put on her shoes. She swung onto her bike, flipped up the kick stand with her heel, and pushed on the right pedal. But the bike felt peculiar – it didn't move. She looked down. Darn! The back tire was flat. She was going to have to walk.

She headed out of the yard and down the street, sniffing

the air. It felt damp on her cheeks and it smelled sweet. she had never been outdoors so early. The sunlight was golden and tree shadows lay long beside the sidewalk. No cars moved on the street. Nobody was outdoors. Chilling Street was strangely quiet.

Suddenly she stopped. What was that?

She looked around. Nothing.

She started walking again, peeking out of the corners of her eyes, listening.

There! There it was again — a scurrying, shuffling sound.

She spun around in time to see something orange disappear behind a tree.

Double phooey!

"Nicki," she called, "you might as well come out. I saw you. Don't try to hide."

Nicki slid around the tree and stood with her back against it, looking sideways at Gabby. She stuck her thumb in her mouth. She was wearing her pajamas and tennies and her Kitty Nose. But she didn't have her robe or a jacket on.

Gabby went to her and tried to sound like a grownup. About the last thing in the world she needed was Nicki tagging after her. "It's too early for you to be out," she said.

"You're out," said Nicki, the kitty whiskers wobbling.

"That's different," said Gabby. "You're not dressed. You're not supposed to be outside in your pajamas."

Nicki looked down at herself. "But I'm all covered up."

"Those are your night clothes," said Gabby. "Come on. I'll take you home." She held out her hand.

"No," said Nicki. She stared at Gabby, unblinking. "I'm going with you to catch a crook."

Gabby tried to take her hand. "Home," said Gabby.

Nicki snatched her hand away and held it behind her. "If you take me home I'll wake up Mommy and Daddy and tell them you're outside when you're not supposed to be because it's still almost nighttime and they'll make you stay in the house forever and ever," said Nicki all in one breath.

Gabby gave in. Nicki clearly had the upper hand. "Here," she said, "put on my jacket." She stuffed Nicki into the jacket and knelt and tied her shoelaces. Then, huddling her shoulders against the cool morning air, she began walking. "I'm going pretty far," she said, "and you can't turn into a baby halfway there and want to come home."

"I'm not a baby. Don't call me a baby," said Nicki.

"Good," said Gabby. It was the first time Nicki had ever said *that*. "And you've got to be quiet and do exactly what I say," she added.

"I'll be quiet as a little cat," said Nicki, trotting along beside Gabby. "Where are we going?"

"You'll see," said Gabby. "Being quiet means not asking questions."

Nicki was still. Gabby could hear her breathing hard as she hurried to keep up. Gabby slowed down a little.

She led the way to the corner, turned onto Lillith Street, and hurried for one block, two blocks, three.

"Are we almost there?" panted Nicki.

"We turn at the alley," said Gabby.

They followed the alley past fences and garages. Gabby counted the garages – two, three, four.

She stopped at the next garage. "Now, you've got to be really quiet," she hissed at Nicki.

Nicki's eyes were round above the Kitty Nose. She pumped her head up and down.

Opening the gate carefully so it wouldn't squeak, Gabby went into the yard with Nicki almost stepping on her heels. The garage had a window halfway down its length. She stood on tiptoe, her fingers on the sill. But she couldn't see in. She wasn't tall enough.

She looked around the yard. A washbasket stood on the back porch.

She put her finger to her lips to keep Nicki quiet, said, "Stay here" softly, and tiptoed to the porch. She brought the basket back to the garage, turned it over, and tested it. Yes, it was strong enough to hold her.

She climbed onto the basket and looked into the garage.

Sunlight from the window on the far wall lit up the inside of the garage. And there, gleaming in the morning light, was the silver ball. Somehow, though, it seemed to be tangled up with other things. Gabby cupped her hands around her eyes and pushed her face right up to the glass.

It took a minute to sort out all the missing things. Yes, there were the shiny planting boxes. And she could, sort of, make out the tree lights. Only nothing was quite the way she had expected anything to be. Imagine how surprised Mr. Oakley and Mrs. McCabe and Mrs. Driscoll were going to be!

Nicki tugged at her sweater. "What's in there?" she whispered hoarsely. "Can I see, too?"

Gabby jumped down from the basket. "You're not tall enough, even with the basket, and you're too heavy for me to lift. Come on. Let's go home. I'll tell you all about it on the way. We've got to get back into the house before Mom and Dad wake up."

13

Gabby Fingers
the Mastermind

"Welcome to the William Sweetman Middle
School. Today is Career Day. We are in Mrs. Cole's
classroom. Betsy Leavis is telling about becoming
a ballet dancer. . . ."

Bucky spoke softly. He sounded just like an announcer
telling about a golf match. He sat by himself near the front
of the room, talking into his tape recorder.

"Amy Braden is now coming to the front of the
class. She's carrying a box with holes in the top
of it."

Amy set the box on Mrs. Cole's desk. "I'm going to be a
vet," she said proudly. "I've got some goldfish. And I've got
a caiman. His name is Louie."

Gabby's ears perked up. Bucky had found his caiman! The trick with caiman food in different places must have worked. She tried to catch Bucky's eye, but he was busy watching Amy.

"This caiman used to belong to Bucky," Amy went on. "And he used to be lost. Yesterday Bucky found him under the laundry tubs in their basement because that's where Bucky put some food like Gabby told him to."

Gabby grinned.

"Bucky's mother said he couldn't keep the caiman anymore. So Bucky gave him to me and I named him Louie." Amy took the caiman out of the box and told how to take care of it. Then she talked about what veterinarians do.

Gabby flipped through her notebook and smoothed the private-eye ad. She was going to just die if Mrs. Cole didn't call on her soon.

Amy's eyes danced. "And there's something even better. An old, old lady moved in at the end of our block. She has this little black poodle and I'm going to take him for walks every day."

How wonderful! Walking someone's dog was almost as good as owning one. Amy could hug it a lot. "You didn't tell me about that," Gabby whispered when Amy came back to her seat.

"I've hardly seen you since Wednesday," Amy whispered back.

"Quiet down, people," said Mrs. Cole. "Let get on with our reports. Mary Lynn?"

Mary Lynn said she was going to dig up dinosaur bones. Tommy Riccio was going to be a football player. Justin said he was going to be a teacher.

Justin? A teacher?

He didn't laugh or make a joke. "I'm going to teach really little kids," he said seriously.

Gabby's mouth fell open.

"I like little kids," he went on. "They're neat." He told about his Uncle Bill who was in college learning to be a teacher.

Gabby was listening so hard, and staring at Justin, that she almost didn't hear Mrs. Cole call her name.

"Gabby O'Brien is carrying a notebook and a sheet of paper. She's holding up the paper. It looks like an ad. . . ."

Bucky's voice was quiet in the background.

Even though everyone knew what she had been doing, Gabby told about being a private eye. She showed the ad and read some of the things in her notebook.

"I followed lots of leads," she said. She had written some of the words private eyes use in her notebook. *Lead. Case. Clue.* She wanted to sound like a private eye. "The case didn't break until yesterday," she said.

Everyone leaned forward to see the notes from the mail-boxes.

She tucked them back into her notebook. "The notes are almost the same, the way they say things. They're on the same kind of paper and the words all look like they were typed on the same machine. That's because they were written on a computer."

Gabby paused for effect.

"I knew where there was a computer — a whole roomful of them. That room is right here at William Sweetman School."

The classroom was still. Even Bucky was quiet. Nobody moved.

"I knew who used the computers a lot," said Gabby. "So this morning I got up really early. I went to a certain house and I looked in a certain garage window, and I saw the planting boxes and the lights and the silver ball. Only that's not what they looked like anymore."

She turned to Porter.

"You know you took all that stuff, Porter Winfield. And you know why. I found out because I'm a private eye. But now you've got to tell everybody about it."

Everyone turned round eyes on Porter.

"Porter!" gasped Mrs. Cole. "What on earth have you done? You wouldn't *steal* things!"

Porter had been sitting with his arms wrapped around a stack of books, his chin resting on the top book. Slowly he unwound himself from the books and chair and stood up. "Didn't steal anything," he said mildly. "I just borrowed the things I needed for today."

"Ladies and gentlemen! Gabby O'Brien, Private Eye, has solved some crimes. The class is going wild. Everyone is talking at once – "

"People! Be still!" Mrs. Cole was usually good-natured. But her voice was sharp now, and she looked upset. "Porter, I hope you have a good explanation."

"Excuse me," said Porter. "I've got to get something out of the janitor's closet."

He left the room. The door stood open. Nobody spoke. Nobody moved.

There was a whirring sound in the hall and Porter appeared in the door. In his hand he held the cord to his skateboard. Behind him, moving with a soft electric purr, came a robot.

"Ohhhhhhhh." Everyone breathed out softly.

The robot's body was made of two upright planting boxes. Its head was a shiny silver ball. Its eyes blinked off and on. So did its mouth and a row of button-lights down its front. It had two arms made out of springs and it wore leather mittens on its hands. It rode on Porter's skateboard.

Porter went to the front of the room, the robot rolling smoothly after him. He turned and faced everyone. "Listen," he said.

The lights on the robot blinked faster. "My . name . is . Al . ex . an . der." The voice came from the robot. It almost sounded like Porter, only it spoke in one flat tone. "I . am . a . ro . bot. I . can . do . a . trick."

Porter tossed two colored balls in the air. The robot caught one in each hand. Then it began to toss them between its hands. Click-clack. Up-down. The robot moved its arms stiffly, and the colored balls moved up-over-down, up-over-down, click-clack.

"Wowwww!" everyone said.

"Now watch," said Porter. He added a third ball.

Alexander caught that one, too. Then he had three balls juggling in the air.

"And another one," said Porter, tossing a fourth ball to Alexander.

Alexander didn't catch it. It fell to the floor.

"Rats," said Alexander's flat voice.

One by one the rest of the balls fell and rolled away.

"Rats," said Alexander. "Rats. Rats."

"Alexander," said Porter, "what happened?"

"You . did . not . fin . ish . pro . gram . ming . me," said the robot. "Fin . ish . pro . grammmmm. . . ." The word droned to a low tone and died.

A giant sigh whooshed through the room as everybody let out their breath.

"You sure made something exciting, Porter," said Gabby. "I guess you're going to be an inventor someday."

"I'm an inventor *now*," said Porter. "I'll be a better one someday."

"How did you make it juggle?" "Why can it only juggle three balls?" Where . . . when . . . how . . . what if. . . . The questions tumbled out of everyone.

Mrs. Cole held up her hand for silence.

"Porter," she said, "quietly and logically tell us why you invented this . . . this . . . Alexander. What purpose does it serve? And in the name of sweet goodness, tell me why you thought you had the right to take – "

"Borrow," Porter said quietly. "I even sent the people letters so they'd know their stuff was okay after Gabby told at lunch the other day how worried they all were."

" – take," Mrs. Cole said in her no-more-nonsense voice, "things that belong to other people."

Porter looked dreamily out the window. "Well, see, I was just walking along on Chilling Street, and I saw these things, and they sort of added up in my head into a robot." He took a deep breath and went on. "I thought I could make the robot just for today and take the stuff back. I could've figured out how to make Alexander juggle four balls, only I didn't have enough time. . . . Next year I'll make a better robot for the science fair."

"Porter," Gabby said firmly, "you've got to go with me to take the stuff back. Mrs. Driscoll and Mrs. McCabe and Mr. Oakley have to know I solved their mysteries."

"And then, Porter Winfield," said Mrs. Cole, "you are to come back to school. You and I are going to have a long talk."

Everyone crowded to the front of the room to look at Alexander.

In the background, Bucky was talking:

> ". . . it's a madhouse. Everyone wants to meet Alexander, the robot. They're asking him questions. He's blinking but he's not talking. Only the mastermind who invented him is talking."

14

Al.ex.an.der Ex.plains

A strange little parade made its way down Chilling Street that afternoon. Gabby and Porter were out in front. Alexander, lights flashing, rolled along beside Porter. Amy and Bucky and Justin straggled after them, laughing and talking.

Mrs. Driscoll and Mrs. McCabe and Mr. Oakley were all working in their yards. One by one they put aside their gardening tools and came to meet Gabby.

"Mercy me!" said Mrs. Driscoll.

"What in the world!" said Mrs. McCabe.

"I'll be jiggered," said Mr. Oakley.

"Mrs. Driscoll, Mrs. McCabe, Mr. Oakley," said Gabby, "I brought—"

"But that's my silver globe!" gasped Mrs. Driscoll.

"My lights!" rumbled Mr. Oakley.

"Could the creature's body possibly be. . . ." twittered Mrs. McCabe.

Porter pressed a button.

"My . name . is . Al . ex . an . der," the robot intoned. "I . am . a . ro . bot. I . can . do . a . trick."

Porter tossed the colored balls and Alexander did his trick, right down to dropping the last ball and saying "pro-grammmmm."

The grownups were speechless.

Before they could say anything, Gabby told how she had solved the mysteries. "Mrs. Cole says Porter has to give everything back and say he's sorry he stole them."

"Didn't steal," Porter said mildly, "borrowed."

"Well now, that's a matter of opinion, my boy," growled Mr. Oakley. "I drive a hard bargain and I figure you'd better put in a little public-service time to make up for the trouble you caused. My grass needs cutting. Tomorrow." He turned to Mrs. Driscoll. "And you, ma'am?"

"Oh, now," Mrs. Driscoll fluttered, "I'm just so glad to have the silver globe back that I—"

"Ma'am!" Mr. Oakley said sternly.

"Well, yes," said Mrs. Driscoll. "Perhaps my grass should be raked before the garden club comes tomorrow."

"Porter, I'll need your help tomorrow planting flowers in these boxes," said Mrs. McCabe.

"Hear that, boy?" Mr. Oakley said, frowning at Porter. "You start at my place at eight-thirty sharp tomorrow morning."

Porter looked more wide awake than Gabby had ever seen him.

"Yes, sir," said Porter.

Then he unwound and unplugged the lights on Alexander and handed them to Mr. Oakley. He lifted off Alexander's silvery head and put it gently into Mrs. Driscoll's outstretched arms. He unhooked Alexander's springy arms and set them on the sidewalk. He knelt and pulled the two planting boxes apart and took a circuit board and a tape recorder and yards and yards of wire out of them.

Mrs. McCabe picked up the planting boxes.

Porter gathered up the springs and wires and things. He stepped onto his skateboard.

"Porter?" said Gabby. "Remember what Mrs. Cole said? She said—"

"I . am . sor . ry . I . caused . you . trou. ble," said Porter in a voice just like Alexander's. Then he rolled away, back the way they had come, back to William Sweetman School, to hear what Mrs. Cole had to say about borrowing-taking things.

"Well," said Mr. Oakley, looking down at Gabby, "you came through just like you said you would, sis, and that's a fact. Now it's time to pay the piper. Let me see . . . you worked six days at twenty-five cents a day. . . . Any expenses?"

Gabby shook her head.

Mr. Oakley dug into his pocket and counted quarters into her hand.

Mrs. McCabe turned toward home. "Stop at the house, Gabrielle," she said over her shoulder, "so I can pay you."

Mrs. Driscoll looked thoughtful. "I'm glad you weren't just playing a game, dear. You're a wonderful private eye, and I must pay you, of course. But I don't have my purse. Please stop at the house for your fee."

"Oh, but I said you wouldn't have to pay me," said Gabrielle.

"I know, dear," said Mrs. Driscoll, "and wasn't that lovely of you! But you worked so very hard, and I am everlastingly grateful, and I insist on paying you." She went home, smiling down at the silver ball.

Bucky and Amy and Justin crowded around Gabby.

"Hey, Gab," said Justin, "know what?"

Gabby looked at him warily. Was he setting her up to Gotcha! her again?

Justin grinned. "I'm sort of glad I didn't have to fish you out of the lagoon," he said.

It was practically an apology.

Maybe Justin did sort of like her. What a funny idea!

15

The Last Laugh

It was a dark and dreary Saturday. Rain had fallen all night, and it was still raining big, splattery drops. Gabby — in her yellow raincoat and boots and hat, carrying her yellow umbrella — was a bright spot of color as she went to meet Amy. Amy came running out of her house wearing a raincoat with little white dogs on it. There were dogs on her umbrella, too.

Gabby and Amy were on their way to the mall.

"I solved all the hard cases," said Gabby, splashing through a puddle. "But I didn't solve the easy one. I didn't find Miss Haliber's umbrella."

"Maybe you'll still find it," said Amy.

Gabby doubted that. "I've looked every single place she went. It just isn't anywhere."

Amy was a good friend. She tried to comfort Gabby. "I don't think you should feel bad, Gab. You did solve the really hard mysteries."

Gabby held out a hand and let some of the big drops of

rain plop into her palm. "Miss Haliber sure could use her umbrella today." She sighed. "She's awfully nice, even if she did laugh at first. She apologized."

"Grownups hardly ever say they're sorry to kids," said Amy.

Amy had just got her weekly allowance. "I'm going to buy a little castle to put in the fishbowl. It must be boring to do nothing but swim around and around in there," she said. "It will be more fun if Morrie and Gloria have something to swim in and out of sometimes."

Gabby fingered the quarters in her pocket. Her pocket was heavy with them. "Yesterday Nicky said she isn't a baby. That's the first time she's ever said that. Last night my mom said she has to start helping with the dishes. She's going to put away the spoons and forks and pans. I'm going to load the dishwasher. Maybe I'll get Nicki an apron that looks sort of grown-up."

Talking, they turned the corner at the Lucky Ducky.

"Look," said Amy. "Hoot and Annie are here, even in the rain."

Hoot was wrapped up in a poncho. Annie sat beside him under an umbrella rigged to the cart.

"Annie's got little boots on!" gasped Amy.

Gabby wasn't looking at Annie's boots. She knew about them. She was staring at the black umbrella Annie was sitting under. She ran to check out the umbrella's handle. It was gold! A shiny, braided tassel hung from it.

"Hoot!" gasped Gabby. "Where did you get this umbrella?"

"Found it!" said Hoot. "Couple of weeks ago. It was just lying out there in the parking lot. Must have fallen out of somebody's car. It's just the thing to keep the rain off Annie."

Gabby didn't have to compare the tassel with the one in her notebook. But she took it out of her pocket anyway, to show to Hoot. "This is Miss Haliber's umbrella. I've been hunting for it all week."

Hoot studied the picture. "Yep," he said at last. He looked disappointed. "Well, I'll have to give it back then, won't I." He spoke to Annie. "Guess you're going to get wet after all, old girl."

Gabby looked down at Annie's getting-gray face. Hoot said she was sort of stiff now, because she was so old. Gabby hated to think of Annie being achy.

But . . . maybe Annie didn't have to get wet. Gabby had an idea. "Wait," she said. "Wait just a minute."

She ran to the This 'n' That Shoppe, the Store that Sells Everything. When she came out, she was carrying an umbrella. "Here," she said, giving it to Hoot, "here's an umbrella of her very own for Annie."

"Now ain't you a good kid!" said Hoot, unfastening Miss Haliber's umbrella from the cart.

"The red even matches Annie's coat," Amy said happily.

Bucky and Justin had come while Gabby was in the This

'n' That. They were riding their bikes in slow circles around Hoot's cart.

"Hey, Gab," said Bucky. "You're some private eye! Can I tape an interview with you?"

Justin spoke before she could answer. "Know something, Gab? There were all kinds of police cars on Lillith Street just now."

Police cars? What was happening?

"I heard two of the officers talking," Justin went on. "They said something about a murder. I wonder if somebody around there got iced."

"A murder! A real mur – " Then Gabby saw Justin's face. He wasn't smiling, but his gray eyes were dancing.

"Justin!" She almost choked on his name.

"Gotcha!" Justin chortled, slapping his knee.

That's when his bike went out of control. It slipped. It slid sideways.

"Jus-tinnnnn?" wailed Gabby as he sailed over the handlebars and landed in a puddle of water. He sat up in the middle of it, grinning.

Be nice to Justin. Gabby could almost hear her mother's voice. *He likes you.*

Gabby stepped over the bicycle and into the puddle. She leaned down and offered him her hand. "Justin," she said sweetly, "let me help you out of this lagoon." And she hardly laughed at all.

About the Author

Dorothy Haas is a native of Racine, Wisconsin, and graduated from Marquette University. She is the author of over forty books for children, many of which were nominated for state awards. Two of her novels, *The Secret Life of Dilly McBean* and *Tink in a Tangle* were American Library Association "Booklist" choice titles. Ms. Haas has been an editor of children's books, but now is a full-time author. She says that she enjoys sharing her "fantasy life" and having the power to "make the creatures of my imagination come alive for children everywhere."

Ms. Haas is an avid traveler and has made numerous trips to Europe. She currently resides in Chicago, Illinois.